ABYSS DIVERS

LOUIS J. FREDA

Abyss Divers

© 2023 Louis J. Freda

ISBN 978-1-66789-368-6

eBook ISBN 978-1-66789-369-3

CONTENTS

CHAPTER 1

WELCOME HOME

The sun sits high on its throne at midday, washing a quiet hill with warm sunlight. Atop the hill rests a lone tree full of green leaves, the trunk just large enough for one person to sit against. On one side of the hilltop is the large never-ending open ocean. On the other side of the hill, a ring-shaped island. The wind comes with a gentle whisper of its pleasant sound, rustling the light-brown hair of a boy sitting asleep at the base of the tree. Here, he dreams of a world far better than this one, with his back pressed against the tree for support, feeling every rough bump, nook, and cranny of the sturdy bark. Far off into the open ocean, a sound beats like war drums from the sky. Steadily, the dark clouds begin encroaching their way to the island. Darkness blankets the sky and water, while the wind whips and flails in short gusts like it had been filled with hate. Down below, the water swells into a rage in all directions. The boy, woken up by the noise and commotion, quietly sighs as his eyes remain shut. Staggering, the boy stands tired, with a huge stretch from the top of his head to the very tips of his toes. Accompanying his stretch was an all too familiar pop in his lower back. Saddened by the change of weather knocking on the door of the island, the boy groans.

"You just have to rain on my peaceful time, huh, weather?" As he opens his tired eyes, they shine blue like the sky itself. "Well, I better get home before Mom gets upset with me."

The boy turns away from the ocean to follow a dirt trail down the gentle hill slope to his home, with the whole island in sweeping view now. The crater-like island stands alone in a vast ocean, self-contained, isolated. The outer hill creates a full circle; without the few exceptions, it would be a perfect walkable circle. At the bottom, in the middle of the island, sits a lake, its size almost an ocean itself. Inside this lake is a small island in the middle, a mocking replica of the parent island around it. Towering the lonely island stands a gate of worn solid stone; sewn into it are bright gold intricate carvings. In the maw of the gate is an eerie darkness that leads into nothingness. This gate defies reality; it should not exist, cannot exist, yet here it stands, a door with no possible way of connecting to an entrance or exit. To those who have never been to this place, it feels alien; those who were not born here, will never feel peace here. However, for the denizens of this place, it is normal; this gate to an abyss is there as a decoration almost. This gate for most is never to be touched or be ventured into. For a very few, it is their everyday life, to find the answers that lie beyond the darkness, to dive into the abyss. Those souls, who feel the pull, who must answer the call against all odds, legends, and endless recounts of horror and death, become Abyss Divers.

One foot in front of the other, the boy leisurely walks down the cobblestoned path, hopping the broken off corners and edges of the old steps and stepping through and over the protruding blades of grass and weeds coming out of the worn-out cracks. Looking out across the open space, the boy can see the island. The island ring neatly divided in half by the end of various buildings, turning into green pastures. The side the boy resides on is a place full of smokestacks billowing out thick streams of black smoke that fills the area like a dense fog. Some smokestacks release pent-up steam accompanied by a loud whistle like a teapot. Some buildings are winding and twisting on each other, each one more crammed atop the other, barely having any space to breathe. Most of the buildings are so close, they use each other as support to hold themselves upright. The poorly held together sheet metal and used scraps of old wood line the decayed buildings. With a constant bang, then a clatter, the giant cogs that protrude from the workshops, kick into motion for a slight turn and come to a sluggish stop. Again, with another bang, the cog moves, only to halt once again—a shanty town of steam and arduous labor. Some cogs spin indefinitely, some are attached to the side of the buildings like an afterthought, while the others are half in and half out of the buildings. The streets are narrow enough to fit two people shoulder-to-shoulder; not many can breathe here between the claustrophobic buildings and dense smog, but they have no option. Only a handful of locations are allowed more space to operate. Places like the market, dock, government offices—very few are allotted this luxury of space.

However, just on the other side, paraded like a trophy few have earned, the other side of the island rests. Lavish green gardens of plants and vegetables and hedges line every fence and detail. Water fountains spill over with crystal clear water, graciously flowing from one fountain shelf to another. Homes are simply large, extravagant, and designed to take up as much space as they could. These homes built with the finest and purest of materials, polished stone walls adorned with gold and silver. Like a sick joke, the contrast could not be any more apparent between them.

The boy was not concerned about dwelling on such things right now, only to get home lest he face his mother's wrath for being outside too late in the day. Descending down the final half of the steps, one foot in front of the other like a marching toy soldier, he heads into the dense smog. With each step, his patched-together shirt of mismatched clothing loosely hangs on him, as if it was made for someone else. All the same, his overalls were buttoned as much as they could be to still be held together. His pant legs rolled up, so it would not be too long for him to trip over. Two different shoes enclosed his feet, one a size too big, the other just a size smaller with the addition of some holes for it to do what he needs it to do, be a shoe. Stepping off the last step, the boy is faced against a wall of homes; he looks left, then right; ultimately he decides to go left. With his hands in his pockets, the boy navigates the winding streets and alleyways, skipping old murky puddles one after another. Avoiding the known dangerous areas, he bobs between conversations of people in the alleyways. Finally, the dark storm clouds reach over top the island. The boy in time makes it home, with enough time to listen to the small pitter patter of the first rain drops as he closes the front door of his home. Following the first drops to make landfall, a sheet of water rains down onto the city.

Inside the home, just in front of the door, a small square landing is used as a space to store shoes so as to not bring mud or dirt into the house. The boy takes off his mismatched and only just held together shoes. He walks into the long hallway that spans the home. From the first door on the left, he hears an all too familiar middle-aged female voice.

"Joseph, is that you?" the woman asks.

"No, Mom, it's Dave," the boy replies.

"Oh, David, welcome home; come here," David's mother beckons.

Letting out a small sigh from his mothers request, the boy knows what's going to happen, but between the embarrassment, he still does it from love. Entering the first room, he comes to a small square room with not much decorating it. The flame of a small oil lamp flickers on a nightstand—one of the two light sources in the room. Against the front outer wall to the left, there's a poorly kept couch riddled with holes and patches. Adjacent to the couch, there's a small circular window just above the boys height. To the right, a table with three chairs sits further into the room in front of a sectioned-off kitchen. In the middle of the room, a middle-aged woman sits on a shaky wheelchair; from waist down, a blanket covers her legs but not long enough to reach her feet. A slight chill enters the boy's spine as he looks at his mothers feet. The lower half of her legs are enveloped in a solid rock-like formations from her feet to the middle of her shins give the appearance of solid stone. The disease comes flooding to David's mind, Statues Disease—a slow encroaching illness, poisoning the people of this town. Shaken from these despairing thoughts, his mother calls him to his side.

"Come, come; stop standing there like you're a statue and give me a hug," David's mother beckons once again.

Embarrassed, David walks over to his mother's side, whose arms are outstretched with a faint smile upon seeing her son. David bends down as her arms embrace him; the warmth he can feel reminds him of the few times he gets to bask in the sun. Being pressed cheek to cheek, he can feel the small wrinkles around her face.

The mother softly whispers the same words he hears every day, "I love you."

She then gives a gentle kiss on David's forehead; leaning back he repeats the same words he says every day, "I love you too, Mom."

Reluctantly she lets her young boy go, unwrapping her arms from around his shoulders, slowly letting them fall to his hands, finally letting go.

As David is now free, he turns to the rest of the open room. He walks to the small, connected kitchen resting in the back corner. This so-called kitchen is furnished with only the necessities. The countertop is short coming up to the boys waist. As short as the countertop is, it is not very long as well; to do any cook work, David must slightly bend over to use the surface. Occupying most of the counter is the sink, off to the left side, butting up against the wall. Directly in the middle is a separate oven with a stove top that cuts up through the countertop. Kneeling down to the far right of the counter, David looks inside a small waist-high fridge, noticing it's lacking in food. He sighs, standing back up in front of the countertop. Next, he rummages around the cabinets, deciding on what to make for dinner while chatting with his mother.

"Do we not have any bread, Mom?" David asks.

"No." Pausing briefly, she thinks, then continues, "Joseph was sent out to get some; it has been a while. I wonder what he could be doing."

Massaging between his eyes in frustration, David groans out, "He's probably off by the dock again, looking at the lake."

"He better not be; you know what that gate does to people," David's mother says with a sharp angry tone.

"I know, I know; it turns people into fools, and only the truly dumb go into there to die," David says in a high-pitched mocking tone as he rolls his eyes, repeating the sentence as it is repeated at every chance it gets to appear.

"Just like your father," David's mother says.

"Just like dad," David repeats, as his tone shifts to a depressing one.

Just as David finishes his comment, the pair listen as the front door can be heard swinging open violently. The whipping wind and torrential downpour of rain battering the outside world is let inside for a small moment. The man who opened the door rushes to close the door immediately as not to let any more rain into the home like an unwelcome guest. A man holding two soaked brown bags with both his arms closes the door with his foot and enters the home. Standing in the doorway to the room, he looks around, huffing and out of breath. Quickly, the man walks over to the tiny countertop; as he drops the bags, they make a wet slap. The path the man took to the counter has left a heavy trail of water as it is falling off him. Sharply, David's mother speaks up.

"Joseph! Your shoes, shoes!" she yells.

Joseph looks down, observing the trail of mud leading from the door to his feet, then hurriedly goes back to the front of the door to take off his shoes. Wet from top to bottom and covered in mud, he places them next to the boy's own pair of shoes, then reenters the room.

"Sorry, Mom," Joseph says.

Joseph begins to take off his overcoat, hanging it up on a stand at the entrance of the room, raveling tattered clothes in the same shape as David's—poorly sewn buttoned-up shirt, all held together by overalls.

Quickly, Joseph greets his mother in much the same fashion as David did but going through the motions much quicker. Joseph walks around the table, into the kitchen; standing next to David, the man is only a head taller than David. He then finds a seat on one of the two stools that stand alone in the kitchen. As he is looking at David, who's now at eye-level, Joseph's features become apparent; he is only a handful of years older. His chin and jawline start to sprout the beginnings of a beard with a more defined out-line of a goatee. The three altogether make it more apparent than ever that they share similar face structures: the same brown hair and bright blue eyes. They only all differ in age. Joseph leans in, whispering to David.

"Dave, let's talk in the other room," Joseph says.

"No," David responds quickly.

"Come on, real quick," Joseph begs again.

"Can it wait until I'm done making dinner and you're done cleaning the floor?" David says as he points to the floor.

"Fine, fine, I have to get out of these cold wet clothes anyway, so I'm looking forward to a nice hot dinner," Joseph says as he stands up.

While pulling the food out of the bags, David waves his hand in the air, dismissing Joseph. Standing up, Joseph has a playful smirk across his face, knowing that soon this conversation will be different now that David has decided to humor him. Joseph leaves the room for a brief moment, then returns with a mop, bucket, and a towel. While David looks over the ingredients, Joseph begins cleaning the puddles of mud and water in the room. As David pulls the food Joseph bought, he racks his brain to try to come up with something edible.

The meager items Joseph could buy with the little money they had is the best they could do. The bread was riddled with multiple spots of green, not enough to throw the whole loaf away. There were bruised vegetables, some growing strange spots; David keeps the ones in edible shape. Lost in thought, he pulls out can after can of stuff as he describes them. Next and what seems to be last, there was meat on the brink of being spoiled.

Looking on in disappointment at the grotesque meat, David sighs, setting it on the counter, everything practically stacked on top of one another. He then stands and ponders about the few dishes of food that would be possible to make. Thinking as best as he can, only one dish comes to mind: stew.

Living on this side of the island is not the best; some don't even calling it living, more like barely existing. Those unfortunate enough to be here can only do what they can. Drawing water into a big pot, David places it onto the stove top to boil it so the water is drinkable. He then begins chopping the meat along with the dented vegetables. His mother speaks up while looking out the window as the rain shows no sign of stopping.

"Do you hate me?" David's mother asks.

As the chopping stops, David replies, "No, of course not, Mom."

"I brought you into . . ." she pauses to gesture to the surroundings, "this world."

"So what? It's hard, I know, but I have you and Joseph," David points to the front door as Joseph is emptying the bucket outside. "And you have Joseph and me."

"Well, if only your father could have seen how you two have grown. You're still young but you look so much like him, and Joseph even more so," David's mother says, smiling.

"I'm sure he's watching from wherever he is." David's chopping continues as the two talk some more. "We'll take care of you, Mom, it's going to be fine. All we have to do is keep working, and we'll save up enough to get you better," David says.

Hearing stern resolution in his voice, David's mother can only smile, confirming with him. "I'm sure you will, but don't forget to take care of yourselves; you two are more important than the old me," David's mother says.

"I will, don't you worry," David replies.

After the final meal preparation, some time has passed; the sun has finally found its resting place below the horizon; the night has come. Across the whole town, the gears start to slow down as the working day comes to an end. The plumes of smoke whittle down smaller and smaller until nothing comes out of them anymore. All over the town, the flickering of oil lamps nestled in their glass housings start to light up. Few shops remain open—some restaurants and bars with people still lingering around.

At the kitchen table sit the small family of three, enjoying their time over the food. The day is winding to an end. Now, at this precise time, a noise rings out across the whole island, a deep bellowing bell sound—three times this bell rings all across the entire island. Once the bellowing subsides, everyone knows what this means. David, Joseph, and their mother look over at each other as they finish their meal. David and Joseph begin cleaning up, putting their plates away and washing the last few plates.

"Six o'clock already, huh!" David mumbles.

Joseph finishes the final cleaning, then says goodnight to his mother. As he walks out the door, he looks over to David—a glace that says, remember I wanted to talk. David stands up from the couch and says goodnight to his mother, then leaves the room. Taking a left down the hallway, David comes to two doors on either side. The one on the right is wide open, letting the bathroom be out on display. David opens the door on the left. This room is much smaller than the first living room, with only two beds just wide enough for one person to sleep on. The two beds are just far apart for one person to stand between them. Against the wall to the left, at the foot of the left bed, is a solitary dresser with four drawers, two for each of the boys. Joseph, already lying down on the right bed, sees David walk into the flickering light of the lone lamp in the room. David, finding his place on the edge of the left bed, is staring at his brother, preparing to shun his idea from the start. Sitting up, Joseph now face-to-face with David, begins whispering, to not let any prying ears hear them through the thin walls.

"Let's go into the gate, Dave," Joseph says with excitement.

"No," David quickly replies.

Putting his hands up to catch his younger brother's hastiness, Joseph says, "Just hear me out on this one." Joseph relaxes, sitting with his back against the wall now. "Once." Joseph points his index finger to the sky. "That's all we need; we go in once, we come out rich, we save Mom, we return to normal lives, slaving away in dead-end jobs in one of these factories."

"Do you know how expensive that cure is for her disease?" David sighs.

"Like a few thousand dollars," Joseph replies.

David, holding his whole face in the palm of his hand, groans, "If you weren't my brother, I would slap you." Looking up, David corrects his older brother, "Millions, it's a few million dollars." Intently staring at the ground, David continues. "Do you really think just going in once will get us enough money? Do you really think we have any skill to survive going in there? Do you even think of things like that first?"

"Nope," Joseph replies.

"I'm not surprised." David's face once again meets the palm of his hands.

"Mom doesn't have long, a few months at best; we both know this," Joseph says as he leans forward.

Looking around the room to quell this uneasy feeling of the truth David already knew but tried to hide from. For the longest time now, David had tried to avoid the harsh truth of the possibility that his mom would die from this disease. All David could do until now was work diligently to earn and save the money needed. David knew his current work is slow, deep down he knew it would never work, but if he just worked harder, maybe it could have all worked itself out. These thoughts raced back and forth, scrambling every inch of his brain. For David, perhaps there was no alternative, no way out. David thought for once, perhaps his brother was correct; their mother would not make it to the next year which was just four months away. He needs money and he needs it now, to buy the cure as fast as possible—such a cruel world they are forced to live in. Finally, David speaks up after intense moments of thought.

"Would District 1 even sell it to us?" David asks.

"They wouldn't care where we came from; money is money to them, over on the other side of the island, whether it came from District 57 or not," Joseph replies.

David raises his head and begins twiddling his thumbs one over the other, once again trying to think of some other way, some safer way; he comes with his final conclusion, "I don't want to die before I'm even sixteen, Joseph," David says.

"And me before I'm twenty," Joseph says.

"So with that, the smart thing to do is research all we can and try to swing the odds in our favor here," David says.

"Right, right," Joseph agrees.

"Let's look into equipment, pricing, facts, and even stories—something, anything to help us get a leg up on this and come out alive." Joseph nods in agreement to David's ideas. "Did you get any of what I just said?" David asks.

"Yes, so we're doing this tomorrow, right?" Joseph replies.

For the third time, David's face has found its place in both the palms of his hands. "No, we don't have money, so let's just work like normal tomorrow and I'll figure out a plan of action," David says.

"That's what I like; I'll head to the dock, to the registration office, and get the forms ready," Joseph says.

"Yeah, yeah, I can't believe I agreed to something you came up with," David mumbles.

"I knew you'd come around eventually; you're as sturdy as that gate itself," Joseph says with a slight chuckle.

"Shut up and go to sleep; I'm tired." Standing up, David blows out the oil lamp hanging over the two.

One last time in the darkness, Joseph speaks up, "We don't have much time, so we'll have to be fast."

David only replies with a small hum of agreement. Down outside of the stalwart gate, time becomes more important than ever; here, time is a currency, time is worth your life.

CHAPTER 2

LOST

S tanding perfectly still, braving the torrent of rain, an older man, taller than most people, with his arms crossed, is watching the open gate. Despite his age, he has kept himself in shape, an old habit. He is wearing a thick, short gray beard; his face is wrinkled and worn from ages of experience. His salt-and-pepper gray hair is short and receding. Old age has stopped the man from doing what he used to do, but time has allowed him to pass on experience. He's dawning a raincoat, covering his whole upper body down to the middle of his shins; it helps shed the rain off. Even in this intense wind and rain, he can still manage to stand in his place; this too he earned from years of work. As the man aged he learned it best to temper his body to be the best it can even now, especially for this line of work. As he continues to stare intently into the open gate, the final toll of the bell rings. Soon after, the ground itself begins trembling all around; some who were still doing busy work around the camp fall or trip. Those who have experience in this can still stand; for the old man, the only part of him that moves is the uneasy tapping of his foot. From a distance, a young woman yells to the man through the rain.

"How many!" she yells out.

The man replies in his deep grizzled tone, "Two."

From the top of the gate, a solid stone slab appears like a wall being lowered down at a constant slow speed. Down the long, dark hallway, two dim lights can be seen swinging back and forth rapidly. Between the two dim lights, a third light appears, as the lights make their way closer to the opening of the gate. Slowly, others surround the old man, curious to peer into the darkness and see what the man is waiting for. As the lights get brighter and brighter, an intense heat starts rising out from the gate. Even the cold icy drops of rain begin to warm up to a lukewarm temperature. Slamming footsteps can be heard now, followed by the clanking of metal on metal. The heat rises and rises; the once cold rain now more akin to a hot shower, fall around the gate. The door, undaunted to meet its resting place on the floor, slowly falls ever so. In the chaos from inside the gate, tired panting starts to rise from the direction of the two lights. Coming into view down the hallway, two men running with a mountain of equipment attached to them. On their backs, backpacks spilling over with metal and various items of value, glass bowels fall to the ground shattering. Scraps of metal pieces clang on top of one another, leaving a trail of items—relics of all kinds, swords of gold, crowns of jewels, coins in all shapes and sizes. The lanterns, strapped to the waists of the men, swing frantically as they rush to the exit in a full-on sprint. Encouragements are yelled down the hall from those on the outside to make it out, to run faster, to keep moving, to not stop. Chasing behind them is the source of the extreme heat in plain view, a wall of fire from corner to corner blocking out the hallway. As the fire races closer, it nips at the men, chasing the backpacks of valuables, consuming the fallen pieces, reclaiming them. The door to the gate lowers even with the men just moments away, moments to salvation, safety. However, the gate too low, the space between the floor and the gate too narrow for a person to fit, the men, just within an arm's reach, make a final desperate leap to the exit, tightly the gate slams shut. The two men's lanterns, once still fueled, snuffed out, engulfed in the wall of flame on the other side of the gate.

The fire has come to its end; it has reclaimed the last of what belonged to it, what it owned. In the harsh rain, sighing and talking resumes in front of the gate, as it had before. The heat slowly dissipates and nothing but stone remains; the cold rain creeps its way back. The old man turns around and walks to a large make-shift tent sitting behind a table. He opens the door flap, entering the tent; inside is a table with paperwork spewed across it. Sitting at the table is a woman studying all of the paper. Standing in front of the woman, the older man speaks.

"Bruce Johnson, Alfred Woods, lost to the abyss," the old man says.

Looking down, the woman finds a piece of paper, studies it, then finds the two names and marks next to them, "LOST."

"May they find peace," the woman quietly whispers. Hunched over the desk, she scans the papers, then adjusts her narrow-brimmed glasses, and picks up two pieces of paper and begins writing on them. "I'll send the reports to the families or any relatives," she says, looking up to the man.

In silence, the older man's only response is a small nod of his head. Turning around, he walks out of the tent; the man enters into the rain again. Around the muddy camp, the noise of work is dying down. Various people light up small oil lamps hanging around on sticks. The older man walks past the few people hanging around; some are just relaxing by a small fire, covering from the rain. Other people are just trying to smoke a cigarette, braving the rain. Walking past a group of men, one speaks up.

"Wanna smoke, commander?" one man says, holding out a slightly bent lit cigarette to the older man.

"No, thanks; I'm heading to bed," the commander replies.

Entering into his small tent and sheltered from the rain now, the commander takes off his soaking overcoat and hangs it to dry on a coat stand. He sheds off layer after layer of clothing, getting to nothing but one pair of pants and white shirt. He then sits at the edge of the cot with nothing more than a pillow and thin blanket. He takes off the worn boots, places them at the foot of the bed, and lays down. As the man lays on his bed staring up at the tent shaking in all directions being battered by rain and wind. He is unfazed by all the noise, finally getting a place to rest, his exhaustion takes hold as he falls asleep.

CHAPTER 3

WORK DAY

As the night passes by, the rainstorm slowly loses all of its energy after assaulting the island for half a day and all night. The clouds start to dissipate. Just as the last cloud dissolves, morning comes. A few straggling stars in the early sky are now getting masked by the slow rise of the sun. The sky that once housed nothing but darkness now shines with vibrant deep purples and streaks of orange as they all merge into endless blue. The sun comes into full view; as the bottom lip of the sun lets go of the horizon all across the island, it starts—the same rhythmic three beats of a deep bell. The day has started, the town begins anew, smoke starts rising from the chimneys. Gears all across the town begin turning, the clanging of metal against metal rings out. All the while, in the middle of the island, the door to the gate begins moving again. Rising in the air, the hefty stone wall shakes the dirt off from the ground, unveiling the same black dark tunnel. Standing at the opening, the commander in front of groups of people await eagerly to begin marching in. The gate slams to a halt; at the top of the gate, the groups of people enter. The commander counts them as they walk in, keeping a personal track of who is entering, as well as who will leave. Burdened by the packs on their backs and freshly lit lamps, the people go into the abyss.

The banging of metal and whistling of steam are being let out now in a full sprint. David finally awakens from his sleep, sitting up in his bed; even with a full night's sleep, David is still just as tired. As he yawns, he begins stretching. Folding back into a normal posture, David turns to sit at the edge of the bed. Looking over at the once full bed next to him, he notices Joseph is gone. Strapping his old worn shoes back on, David stands up, ready to take on his day of work. He rubs the back of his neck, wondering what made him agree to Joseph's demand last night. Although Joseph's words did bare truth, David did not like them. Even now, David feels no good might come of this but decides to cling to the hope that maybe it just might all work out. He walks across the hallway into a small bathroom that housed nothing more than a sink, toilet, and a drain in the corner that nearly passes as a shower. David then takes a quick moment standing at the toilet to relieve himself, still thinking about last night. Suddenly, an almost defining bang is heard. What felt like the whole earth had moved, stopped just as fast as it had happened. The movement showers David in dust, and a small piece of debris from the ceiling bounces off his head onto the floor. He could only think this: he cannot hope that this plan works out, he has to make it work, no matter what happens or what stands in his way. Leaving the bathroom, dusting himself off like some old furniture, he walks past the large open room. Looking in to check on his mother, he sees that she is surprisingly fast asleep in her wheelchair. Letting out a small, surprised huff, David murmurs.

"Isn't that something."

David opens the front door to the tight alleyway. Standing there, he takes in the view of all the wet cobblestone walkways and the buildings dripping from last night's rain. He starts his walk through the rows of buildings packed haphazardly and tightly beside each other, some rising into the sky at most four floors tall. The tightly packed buildings allow just enough light into the alleyway. However, the buildings are tall enough that the morning sun is blocked from all angles until midday. Walking down the alley, David sneaks around the corners, over piles of trash and debris and past people hanging about where they can. He finally makes his way to a metal gate, hanging from which a sign reads "Production District 36."

Here, the alleyways open to full-on streets as the delivery trucks need space to drive. All kinds of materials that the divers in the gate come out with are being delivered. As dangerous as the gate is, it acts as the heart of this entire island, a type of necessary evil. Without the gate number one, not even the rich can get so much as a scrap of metal.

During work hours, factories roll open their large doors, allowing workers and deliveries to come and go. David reaches one such factory; the air is filled with more noises than one could count—whistles, clanging, various machines working, material shifting clashing, even people yelling from one to another. David gazes up at the walkways going from place to place and stairs up and down to different levels of floors. Conveyor belts from a delivery space of the factory stretch out like a plate of spaghetti. Some belts go through walls, then under a giant crane using a claw that grabs a full hand of metal. Once up into the air, the arm rotates and drops the metal onto other conveyor belts. This is a factory in full motion, working in sync, perfectly timed. David walks through the work going on around him, passing belts lined with people working on them. Some people manually pick up pieces of metal and sort them into metal boxes besides them. Other people come to collect the full boxes, replacing them with new empty ones. As David walks, he enters a closed off room and sees a man seated at the desk. The man's shirt is mostly clean, with only a handful of stains here and there. His hair only adorns the sides of his head, while his face is old and worn and wrinkles line every corner of his face. He takes a puff of the cigar in his mouth, then looks up from the paperwork and greets David who's just walking through the door.

"Davey, how was your day off yesterday?" the man says.

"It was good for the most part, Mr. Johnson," David replies.

"Good, good; how's your mother doing? I know she's sick, that's why you keep working hard," Mr. Johnson says.

"She's getting along." David turns to a clock on the wall with small name cards hanging below the clock.

"Have you seen your brother? He hasn't clocked in today yet. Is he working somewhere else?" Mr. Johnson asks.

As David picks up the card with his name on it, he can't help but think of the new plan they have set in motion behind the scenes. "Not that I know; he probably got distracted by something," David says.

The man lets out a small chuckle. "Joey has a habit of being a free spirit, that's for sure, but you, I like you; you work hard, that's good," Mr. Johnson says as he points to David with his two fingers holding the cigar.

As he sets the name card into the clock, it rings a little bell, followed by a small noise of the clock's inner workings moving, stamping the card with the current time. "Thanks, I'm just trying to get by, for my mom." Turning to the door, David starts to leave the office.

"By the way, Davey, do a good job today too." Mr. Johnson gives a small wave to David as he walks out the door.

As David walks around the factory to his usual spot of work, he can't help but think, how do people act so nice yet care so little? All of Mr. Johnson's words were nothing, just hollow imitations of speech. They carry no weight, David knew this very well. David walks into that office every day and has the same conversation like clockwork; Mr. Johnson doesn't care. All he cares about is the money all the workers make him. David knows this, he sees it every day; he lives it. David watches those that get hurt and can no longer work get thrown to the street, without a second thought, on the spot. David's thoughts get interrupted as he is walking up the stairs to a different level. He looks down at the entrance and sees Joseph run through the door. Joseph quickly stops to a fast walk in front of the office. David notices Joseph stuffing papers into the inside pocket of his jacket. Sighing, David continues to his work spot between two much taller adults standing over a conveyor belt sorting trash from valuables. Across from David on the other side of the conveyor belt, another young boy of around David's age is also sorting out the same trash.

The boy notices David, then looks up and gives a short wave. His small hat covers the top of his head and forehead as he looks back down. His clothes are identical to David's, only for the difference in color. David, standing adjacent from the boy, greets him back, as he looks down now at the trash moving to one side.

To David's left side is an opening that goes straight down a garbage shoot, the ultimate end for the trash on the conveyor belt. Without looking up, the two boys start to talk over all the noise; the boy with the hat starts off greeting David.

"You enjoy yer day off yesterday, Dav?" the boy says.

"As best as I could, Sean," David replies.

"Good thing ya weren't here anyway," Sean says.

"Why, what happened?" David asks.

"Ya know old Brian right, up on level three C?" Sean says as he points upwards briefly.

"Yeah, what about him?" David asks.

"He tripped." Sean makes a whistle sound, then takes one hand above his head and lowers it back down to the conveyer belt. "Splat."

"Oh, damn!" David grimaces.

"A real show, I tell ya; hit one of them steam pipes and tumbled to that ground," Sean says.

"Did his family pick up his body?" David asks.

"Naw, couldn't afford that service, so maintenance left his body outside, trash collectors took him," Sean says.

"That's rough," David says as he shakes his head.

"But, hey, besides that, at lunch, me and some of them boys are going to that dock and hanging about; ya going to come?" Sean asks.

"No, thanks, I'm going to keep working," David replies.

"Hey, don't hurt me feelings like that, we all think ya need more than one day a week off, Dav; take a lunch once in a while, huh," Sean says, insisting.

"I'll think on it, Sean," David replies.

"Bah, stop thinking all the time; just do, would ya?" Sean waves his hands at David dismissively.

As the mundane workday drags on, a very distinct whistle can be heard throughout the whole factory. The conveyor belts come to a full stop, a majority of the people working have stopped and begin walking away from their positions. Lunch has started; a choice for the workers, one unpaid hour to eat, or use the time to continue working. It is a choice David forgoes all the time to make that little bit of extra money. Today is no exception; walking to the ground level where the giant claw picks up heaps of metal, dropping it into a pile, extra work can be found here. Metal is sorted into usable or décor; useful metals from steel to copper are separated into their own pile. Valuable metals like gold and silver also are shoved to the side, into their own pile. As David crouches down to examine some pieces to be sorted, a familiar voice comes approaching from behind.

"Dave, Dave!" the voice shouts.

Letting a sigh escape, David hangs his head to the ground; he knows what's coming. Joseph runs to a screeching halt at David's feet, holding a stack of papers. "Dave, I got them; I got the registration papers to go to the gate," Joseph says, holding the papers up to David.

"Joseph, what happened about researching what to do first?" David says as he lowers Joseph's hand out of his face.

"I did," Joseph says.

"And?" David asks.

"And, I researched we needed to get registration papers and fill them out first," Joseph says.

An audible slap of David's hand meeting his own face can be heard. "Did you find out anything about this, you know, the stuff we'll need, equipment, money, maybe even advice?" David asks.

"Some," Joseph responds.

"Some?" David repeats as he lifts his head.

"Yes, so first off, Dave, ships go to the island every day," Joseph says.

"Joseph, just hanging out at the dock, you can find that out; that is not helpful," David says.

"Or you could even stay on the island to be some of the first to get in," Joseph finishes his thought.

"Wow, Joseph, at least you got something," David says in a surprised tone.

"Ha, see I found something helpful," Joseph says.

"I wasn't serious," David says as his face goes back to a blank slate.

"Well, that just hurts." Joseph chuckles. "And I even looked into the diver store," Joseph continues.

"How expensive is all that stuff?" David asks.

"I'd say, one week is all we need to save as much as possible and we can buy a belt, lantern, and a backpack," Joseph says.

"Is that all that is in the store?" David asks.

"No, they had all kinds of things, small head lamps, different kinds of backpacks, from small to huge, clothes, supporting items like back braces, and even some cool belts. It's weird, they even had swords," Joseph says.

"Swords?" David asks.

"Yeah, swords; everything else I understand but not them," Joseph says, shrugging.

"Did you ask the person working there about them?" David says.

"How late to work did you want me to be? I only had time to look, not ask," Joseph replies.

"That's something we should look into; after work, I'll find someone with experience in the gate or maybe even find a book," David says, letting his thoughts out.

"See, Dave, with your brain and my . . ." Joseph begins waving his arms around his head as he gets stuck in thought. "Bronze, right? No ,what was that word?" Joseph finishes.

"Brawn, Joseph, brawn," David replies.

"Yeah, that, we can do anything together, but before, that sign here." Joseph pulls out a pen and hands the paper to David. Following Josephs pen its pointing to a dotted line at the bottom. "Got to have your signature to get officially recognized as a diver," Joseph says.

Hesitant, David looks at the paper, uneasy about the whole thing, but what gives David some relief is looking back up at his brother who's standing there gleefully with a smile. Joseph's grin from ear-to-ear screams determination; with that little bit, it gives David some hope that this will work and he signs the paper.

"Great, Dave, I'm going to run these down to the office. I should be back before lunch is over." Joseph stands back up, then runs off to the door. David can do nothing but give a small wave as Joseph leaves.

As David resumes his work, the day goes on as usual—the same monotonous day goes on. Standing, sorting, small talk here and there, short glances at the clock to see the minutes tick by. Eventually, the time comes; three loud bangs on a bell can be heard—it's now six o'clock. Everything winds down to a halt; the workers march to the various offices of their respected managers to the same clock on the wall. They pick up the same card, insert it into the clock, then out at the same time. One by one, they leave in groups or in a single line to go wherever they please. As the last person leaves the factory, two people roll the doors to a close, then turn the lights off. The steam and smoke die down; everything has come to the end of the day.

Walking home, David trails behind Joseph as they talk, coming to the large metal gate that houses the production district sign on it. This side of the sign, as they leave, reads "Housing District 57." Passing a dimly lit alleyway, David notices a man lying with his back against the building and his knees pressed up into his face as he sits on the ground. At a quick glance, David notices a patch on the man's shoulder, but it was too dark to see clearly; however, it caught his eye regardless. Joseph calls to David, wondering what has stopped him; snapping out of focus, David regains his senses, then catches up to Joseph. David just tells Joseph that he thought he saw something, but it was nothing. The two reach their destination, home, as they go through the same routine as yesterday. Greeting Mom, having dinner, cleaning up, then going to sleep—same as yesterday, same as tomorrow. David attempts to sleep; he scans his room thinking, looking over at Joseph who's fast asleep, snoring and half covered by his blanket. David can only think of all kinds of scenarios about the gate: what lies in it, what makes it a high reward. These thoughts do nothing but keep David awake. Finally, David sits up, straps his shoes on, and sneaks out of his bedroom. Joseph, despite being only an arm's reach away, is undisturbed by David's movement. David walks out of his room; as he passes the living room, he looks in, seeing his mother in her wheelchair, just as asleep as Joseph.

David thinks to himself, If only I could be as lucky as them to sleep.

He opens the front door gently so as to not make any sound or disturb anyone. He has successfully sneaked out of his own home.

CHAPTER 4

INFORMATION

Walking the street at night has a particular uneasy feeling to it; the air, despite all its flaws with soot and ash, feel better than the stagnant air in the bedroom. Coming to the alleyway as before during his walk home, David sees the same man in the same position as before, frozen in place. David begins approaching the old man; after just one step, the man quickly looks over at David, as if he didn't exist until this moment. David's eyes and the old man's meet for a brief moment. The old man's eyes look hollow, sunken in, as if he has lost all life. Feeling a strange tension in the air, David politely tries to break it by introducing himself. However, the old man doesn't even bother acknowledging David, but instead turns his head back to the side, resting his head on his knee and groans. Despite feeling unwelcomed, David's curiosity gets the better of him; as he gets closer, he notices more of the man's features: his thick cotton jacket, his right sleeve tied up into a ball, what once housed an arm, no longer has an occupant.

Glancing down, David realizes the same can be said about his pants. The old man's right leg was gone; nothing but his thin green-gray pants tied around a stump just below his waist remain. Close enough now, David can make out the patch poorly sewn onto the right shoulder that had caught his attention before. Now, under some dim light, David is able to read it out, "Gate Exploration Team 658." Knowing this now, David can piece everything together—the ragged decrepit old man used to be an abyss diver. Kneeling down next to the old man, David's mind floods with questions, hoping the man has answers to them. Struggling to figure out where to start David hesitates as he gets lost in the mountain of questions, until the old man speaks up in an old, worn rugged voice.

"What you want, kid?" the man asks.

Stumbling over his response, David replies, "Th-the patch, I noticed the patch on your arm; you were a diver, right?"

Letting out a small, annoyed moan, the man replies, "Yeah, what about it?"

"I can't stop thinking about the gate and the abyss; what's in it?" David asks.

"HA!" the man laughs. "What's in it? What isn't in it is the better question," the man says.

"What isn't in it?" David repeats.

"Ooh, yes, what isn't in it is what's in it, everything yet nothing," the man says.

"Now you lost me," David says.

"Lost," the mean repeats in a sullen tone. "Yes, we all get lost eventually."

Looking at the man who seems to begin talking to himself under his breath, David wonders if this might have been a bad idea. But David's thoughts are suddenly interjected by the old man speaking up.

"It all depends on who you ask, curious one; the abyss caters to all needs; it can be whatever you want." The man pauses to take a deep breath and begins once again. "Those who brave the darkness and flames can come out better because of it, BUT we all have a rope and no one's rope is unlimited. Eventually, we all get to the end of it; no matter how rich the abyss makes you, it will pull you in to collect its dues. All of us owe the abyss; whether we know it or not, we all form a connection to it, and it will take what we owe it. Either fast and direct or it will take it slow and wait until we all return to its cold embrace," the man finishes.

David is trying to calm the ramblings of the old man so he can get useful information out of him to answer his questions. "Ok, ok, your philosophy about life was nice, but what is in the gate? What is in the abyss itself?" David asks once again.

Pausing for a moment, the man begins to shutter; he turns his head once again, looking at David straight in the eyes. Earlier, the old man's eyes were empty husks; however, now they fill up with intense fear as he whispers out, "Darkness incarnate." Quickly the man brings his left arm down to his waist and makes a movement as if to turn something on that is no longer there, then continues. "Don't let the lamps go out; they aren't just so we can see. The lamps keep you alive from IT. The darkness itself is alive; only the light can keep it away."

David thinks about the genuine fear in the man; it feels as if something lives in the abyss. Interrupting the man again, David asks, "What about the swords, do they stop it?"

Bursting into laughter, the man responds, "STOP! Ha, nothing stops it, just a tool to keep it away from you, a sense of safety to let people keep going in. The real weapon is the light; the darkness cannot live in it and will do anything to get rid of it."

Trying to keep the man's thoughts straight, David keeps leading him around the conversation. "And the treasure that can be found inside?"

The man goes silent as he looks back at David. "Ooh, yes, the great piles of glimmering treasure; there's enough in there to satisfy all of us; all we have to do is borrow it."

"Borrow it, not take it?" David asks.

"Yes, borrow; the darkness is greedy and wants to keep what is its, but just like us, it all returns to the abyss one way or another," the man says.

"But it can make us rich, right? It can quickly get us money that we need, right?" David asks.

"Unimaginably." The man begins mumbling to himself once more, now lost in even more thought than before. He is just repeating to himself about gold, silver, and darkness.

David believes he has reached the end of this conversation; the man has gone somewhere else entirely. As David stands up to leave, for one last time, the old man speaks up, "Before you go into the abyss, remember you already owe it for your future transgressions against it."

Halting, David stands there, asking the man one last thing, "How did you know I was going in? I never said anything about it."

The man looks blankly at the floor. "I see it in your eyes; once you go in, you change, you can see it in others. We all deep down want to go to the abyss; some are better at hiding it than others." Then one last time, the man starts repeating to himself, "Keep the light on, keep the light on, keep the light on."

David knows this conversation is over and leaves the alleyway feeling slightly depressed now after been given a glimpse of what the abyss can do to people. The man has been an example of what too much time in the abyss will do, a mental note David will remember to keep. Regardless of the dangers present, David has to do this to save his mother, and he is willing to even go into the abyss to achieve that. Equipped with this small sum of knowledge, David makes the trek back to his home, sneaking back into his bed without disturbing anything or anyone. Lying back on his bed, his room somehow still feels stale. As David stares at the crumbling ceiling, a determination comes to him. Just thinking that things have to change, will not make them change. David knows, if he wants to save his mother, he has to make things change. As the night ticks on, David eventually finds himself falling asleep.

CHAPTER 5

PREPARATION

Day after day, David and Josepsh soulless week of work drags on with the event of going into the gate approaching the horizon. David and Joseph continue living out the dull week, saving what little money they could possibly put aside. They'd wake up, go to work, and come home, buying as little food as possible but enough to not make their mother suspicious of them, all the while, still feeding themselves the bare minimum. Until finally, what felt like eternity, the week has come to its conclusion. One last payday stands before the two. After the whole week, the pair has saved enough money to get them started, one whole hundred dollars. Nothing more than dreams and determination. The night of this last payday, they decide to go down to the diver store at midnight so as to not raise any sort of suspicion from their mother.

As the night has come into full swing, everything has gone silent and everyone has fallen asleep. The brothers break out of their own home and head down to the dock; a strange unknown world to David awaits down there. He had never gone down to the docks before. The only places David has gone to were the local shopping district just before the dock, the factory, and up the old cobblestone path to his own little resting place.

Joseph confidently leads his younger brother down through the winding alleyways and under arches that connect the homes together, around corners, slight bends, and past intersections of other alleyways, until they reach their destination. A small shop is still lit up in the darkness of the night, right beside the dock. The front entrance stares back at them and the city on the hill. Being this far down to eye level with the water puts the whole island into perspective for David.

Looking around the water, everything is put more clearly now, the way the crater island takes shape sloping up in all directions. The wooden dock, if not for a few missing pieces for the district organization, would make a complete circle around the water. Following the cliff off the dock, David peers into the water; despite being an enclosed lake, it still moves and sloshes around as if it were controlled by the ocean's currents. Dim lights decorate the island from side to side; one light on all the docks gives David the assumption that they are the same store in the same location as the one in front of them. Turning around, David looks back up to the hilltop to see the big tree that normally towers over David, from down here it looks so small that if he didn't know it was there, he would never see it. Scanning around, he tries to check on his own house; from behind him, Joseph speaks up.

"You can't see it from here," Joseph says.

Curiously, David asks, "What?"

Knowing what his younger brother would do from the very start, Joseph continues his statement, "You can't see our home from here; it's blocked by the building, but it's there, don't worry." Joseph waves his hand, beckoning to David to follow him. "C'mon, let's go in."

Turning away from the hillside had a strange, unnerving feeling for David; however, he pressed on anyway. Following the back of Joseph, they enter the store. A small bell rings out that is hung above the door, alerting any shop worker that a customer has entered. In most cases, the worker would greet whoever has entered. However, in this case, it had awoken a young girl fast asleep at the front desk.

Jolting straight up, the girl quickly tries to rub the tiredness away from her eyes, then fixes her store uniform to flatten any wrinkles, and then straightens her long brown hair. She gives a small clasp of her cheeks from her hands in an attempt to wake herself up. The girl, sitting there, finishes her preparations; completely discarding the fact that just a minute ago she was asleep, she greets the two standing in front of her.

"H-Hello, welcome to diver store number thirteen, w-we've got everything you need, from lamps, jackets, belts, boots . . ." the girl says politely. Quickly, she glances down at the desk to read a paper and continues, "A-and hats, backpacks, and helmets."

The two boys stare back at the young girl; as she finishes her sentence, a small look of pride fills her face with a small smile, as if she had accomplished something quite difficult. With a small amount of awkwardness in the air, David speaks up to break the tension a little bit.

"Hello, we're here to take a look at the diving equipment and probably buy some," David says.

Following soon, David's elbow nudges into Joseph's rib to get him talking. "Right, hi, we just want to look around," Joseph says.

The girl nods, then speaks up again, "O-of course, my name is Jamie, j-just let me know if you need anything."

The two boys simultaneously nod and affirm her that they will. As the two separate, they start to look at the various things hanging on the walls and some of the standing racks in the middle of the floor. Joseph's first choice to look at is the barrel of swords placed in the far corner of the room. The barrel itself looks old and worn—parts of the wood are deeply scratched, splinters line it from top to bottom, holes scattered throughout every plank that make up the barrel. Holding these few pieces of wood from collapsing are two metal bands, one just above the middle of the barrel and one just below the middle. They would have been perfectly spaced if not for the years they have accumulated that now make them slightly off-set and heavy with rust. As for the swords inside the barrel, in opposition to the barrel itself, they look brand-new, glinting with a new enticing shine to them. The handles are perfectly wrapped in polished leather, the cross guard new and ready to protect the wielder's hand. At the end, the pommel, a perfectly shaped ball, is ready to offset the weight of the sword and make it perfectly balanced.

Opposite Joseph, David intently stares at the wall of lamps, one hand resting on his chin as he thinks through the different types of oil lamps. The wall contains sections of all kinds of lamps, from very ornate and detailed to fat wide lamps and skinny tall lamps. All differing in use, some have larger oil reserves to burn longer, allowing a diver to stay in the depths for more time. Some have different wicks, allowing different burning intensi-ties; the range of light settings allows the user to choose what would best suit their need. The labels on the wall around the lamps offer warnings about the usage of them. To make the light brighter to see more burns more oil. To burn the light at a lower setting dims the light but allows for more oil. Ultimately David chooses the simplest and cheapest of the lamps, a lamp that doesn't stand out, a mass-produced lamp. David can only think that he should probably get two, thinking Joseph might not even come over here to look.

After handling the lamps, David moves down the aisle to the sec-tion with backpacks, taking a moment David looks back down the aisle to see Joseph, sword in hand browsing the hat selecting. David only sighs. The backpack section, just like the lamp section, has a wide variety of backpacks. Some large with multiple straps for support, some just small enough to fit on a person's back. They vary in detail and little in function; overall, the backpacks all serve the same use. However, to separate them, some advertise double stitching, a handful go up to triple stitching. Some larger ones boast multiple pockets to store items. A handful of backpacks appear very detailed forgoing function for showboating with the purpose of impressing other divers. But as David's eyes fall to the lower section of cheaper backpacks, he picks one up and tries it on, checking the fit and the price tag and examining the potential spots to hang the lamp from and how easy it is to quickly remove. How easy it is to take off, then put back on, how well it is to quickly stash any findings into the back of it. David goes through a few of them, before deciding on a pair. He walks back to the counter, holding the two backpacks and lamps in both arms. David so far has thought of nothing but the necessities.

Coming to the foot of the counter, David heaves the equipment onto the table. Just then, Joseph comes walking over, dawning a large, exquisite hat and a long over-the-top jacket with all sorts of fancy stitching and tassels. Joseph holds a brand-new cleanly iron-pressed shirt in one hand, and in the other, a sword. Looking him up and down, David rubs his forehead seeing Joseph's appearance. Behind the counter, Jamie lets out a small giggle at seeing Joseph stand there.

"We only have one hundred dollars; put all that stuff back, Joseph," David says.

Joseph, a little disappointed, boos at his brother but turns and goes to put everything back where they belong. Jamie begins putting the prices into the large metallic cash register with loud clicking and clacking as she presses the buttons to manually enter in the price of each item. Ultimately coming to a total of eighty-two dollars, David pulls out the money that he had hid in his pocket. Joseph yells from the sword barrel to the girl, "Just how much the sword costs?" She thinks for a brief moment, then looks at another small piece of paper and exclaims that the swords cost seventeen dollars. Excitedly, Joseph looks down the aisle at David. Quickly doing the math, David knows this will leave them with one last dollar as change. He is offput by the idea of buying something so unnecessary from the start; however, in an attempt to please Joseph, David agrees to buying the sword.

Now that all is said and done, Jamie takes the weirdly stacked and slightly crumpled up dollars that add up to ninety-nine dollars. She quickly counts them to ensure that it is the correct amount of money. After the counting finishes, she looks at the pair and thanks them for coming to the store, handing them two hand-sized containers that read oil.

Curiously, David asks, "We didn't buy that."

"I-it's story policy that anyone who buys their first lamp, g-gets the first fill of oil for f-free," Jamie says.

Excited, the pair stand there thanking Jamie—a crucial part that had been overlooked. David was too preoccupied with buying the lamps but not the oil itself. The two collect their belongings, one oil lamp and one backpack for each of them. They walk out the store with a small sense of pride with them, their equipment bought and ready. Heading back up the alleyway they came through, they talk about all the stuff the store housed. David is intrigued by all the equipment and items. Joseph is more concerned about Jamie than any other item in there.

"Hey, Joseph, if we can get some spare money from all this, maybe we can buy you all those clothes you wanted," David says.

"Maybe, do you think she liked them?" Joseph asks.

"Who? The girl at the desk?" David asks.

"Yes, Jamie; she laughed, right? So maybe she liked them," Joseph says.

"Or, she thought you looked like an idiot," David says.

"Maybe, but that's the first step to get through the door. You need that establishment of character, make yourself stand out," Joseph says.

"Joseph, what are you talking about?" David says.

"Well, you might be just a little too young, but you'll know one day, don't worry," Joseph says as he pats David's back.

Confused, David decides to just let it go. "Anyway, did you think about where we are going to keep this stuff?" David asks.

"I have a friend," Joseph replies.

"Oh, a friend, he says," David says mockingly.

"Yes, a friend; he's planning on coming to the gate with us so he got himself some gear too; so we can keep it with him," Joseph says.

"Great, great, and how will we get to and from our new factory?" David sarcastically asks.

"New factory?" Joseph asks.

"What, you really planned on telling Mom that we just happen to find a bunch of money lying around, instead of getting a new job somewhere with better pay?" David asks.

"Ahh, I see now what you're getting at; that's good idea, but which district though, and how?" Joseph asks.

"We can tell her that Mr. Johnson felt sorry for our situation and decided to put in a good word for us. Something like production district twenty-five as a helpful reward for all the hard work we have put in," David says.

"You think Mom will actually believe that we managed to get from thirty-six to twenty-five because of a good word?" Joseph asks.

"Look, it's just a shot in the dark; if Mom doesn't ask how, we don't tell her. But if she does, we just tell her people have connections all over the place, and a good word can go a long way, that's all," David says.

"That sounds like you should stop hanging out in the library on some of your days off," Joseph says mockingly.

"Well, one of us has to have some sort of a whole brain," David says.

"And us two halves make a whole, right, Dave?" Joseph says.

"Well, at least you got that much going," David replies.

Stopping at an intersection, Joseph looks up at the rusted metal street signs with the names; he then urges David to follow him down a different route. Winding down a new set of alleyways, the brothers come to a house, one similar to David's house—similar to all the houses everywhere for the most part. As Joseph knocks on the door, a man opens it; he looks around the same age as Joseph. They talk quickly and Joseph hands him the gear he had been carrying, then he turns to David.

"Here, give me your stuff; this is Mike," Joseph says.

In the darkness of night, it's hard to see his full face, but trusting Joseph, David hands over his stuff to him, who then hand it to Mike. Joseph says his thanks, then the two depart from there, heading home.

Curious, David asks, "So that's your friend coming along?"

Nodding, Joseph replies, "Yup, he works in the factory over from ours; I met him during lunch, and we got along."

"Ok, then," David murmurs. "Can you trust him to hold onto our stuff, let alone come along into the gate with us?" David asks.

"Yea sure, I think," Joseph replies.

Coming out to the usual route to get home, they continue their journey, passing the same piles of trash around the same bends and narrow alleyways. The two eventually reach home, and with the same stealth as before when leaving the house, they enter it just the same, cautious of each step, making sure not to disturb even the smallest floorboard. Crawling into bed, the two give each other a look of readiness. Tomorrow, the registration will be completed and the very next day, the stage will be set. Two days from now, they have a chance to finally be free.

CHAPTER 6

LIBRARY

Lazying about on top of the hill under the tree, David sits, reading the ending of another book. Standing in front of David, Joseph is swinging his new sword in all kinds of directions. Up, down, left, right, any which way Joseph can move the sword, he tries. After one swing, his hands get caught on each other, letting the sword slip from them and land on the ground with a clang. David, hearing the commotion, looks up for a moment from his book to see Joseph picking his sword up.

"Shouldn't you be resting? We worked tirelessly all week," David comments.

"Well, shouldn't you be training? The abyss is no joke; it's supposed to be really dangerous," Joseph replies in a mocking tone.

David holds up the book he is reading to show to Joseph, "That's what this is; it's old notes from past divers about the abyss, what they found, what they did, all that stuff."

"So you're putting knowledge first and safety second," Joseph says as he begins swinging once more.

"I'm prioritizing knowledge to get a better understanding of what we are getting ourselves into," David says as he begins reading again.

"Oooh, mister smarty farty pants," Joseph mocks in a high pitch voice. He chuckles at his comment along with David for a brief moment.

"Well, look at it this way; you be our injudicious fool and I will get us out of trouble," David says in his own high and mighty tone.

"Inju-what now?" Joseph asks.

"It means you're stupid," David replies.

Joseph turns to face David, pointing his sword at him playfully. "Hey, you can call me indigenous."

"Injudicious," David corrects Joseph.

"Yeah, that, but you can't call me stupid, stupid," Joseph continues.

"Then read a book," David says as he closes his book having finished with it. "Anyway, I have to go return this, and I might check out another one. So I'm going to head to the library, Joseph."

Joseph stretches for a moment. "Yeah, I guess I'll go hang out at the store; see if Jamie is there."

Walking down the old steps, David leads as Joseph follows him and their conversation changes to idle chatter—things like the weather, the city, what's in the abyss, even some plans on how to keep this all a secret from their mother. Stepping off the last stair at the bottom, Joseph peels off, giving David a casual "See you later." David, now free from Joseph, makes his way down the alleyways back to the last district, District 61. Life is already harsh enough in District 57, surprisingly it gets worse from here. In only four districts, all sense of civilization breaks down completely. Here, the buildings that remain are nothing more than empty husks; the people residing in them are just as much empty, both physically and men-tally. Food is scarce here but water is plentiful, only due to it gathering in the deep holes in roads and alleyways. The people lining the alleyways are merely flesh and bone, eyes sunken into their skulls. This place with all its flaws would be dangerous, if the inhabitants had the energy to steal any-thing from anyone. Passing abandoned factories that have been reclaimed by time and age, David makes his way to an opening in this mess. Housed in this opening, a large old ornate building stands, its architecture vastly differs from the buildings around it. The building, despite being old and worn and dotted with a few holes, holds itself up quite well. Looking it over, David always gets this strange feeling about the building, a feeling like it doesn't belong. David can never shake the feeling; it's almost as if the building had come from somewhere else entirely.

Cracking open one half of the front doors, David steps through, into a large open room. Looking up at the building still amazes David. How can a building be so wide and tall yet hold itself up? No other building anyone has made on the island can do this; every other building needs a large system of supports. Also, the inside cannot be open, they need floors, something to give it structure. While walking, David bumps into what is being used as the front desk, shaking him out of his stunned awe. This commotion startles the person behind the desk, causing a thud to come from underneath it.

"Ow, ow, ow," a young girl softly cries out. Standing up from behind the desk, the girl in pain stands before David. A girl, just about the same age as David, perhaps just slightly older, rubs the back of her head that's covered with short black hair. The girl brushes the dust off her slightly tan arms, then moves onto the dust on her patched-up overalls. Situating herself, she fixes her large glasses, her cheeks and nose dotted with freckles, upset from being startled she pouts. "Who's making all that noise, scaring me?" she attempts to yell but keeps her tone hushed.

"Hey, Alice, its' me," David says as he waves to her.

"Oh, David, what can I do for you?" Alice asks.

"I'm here to return the book I borrowed, and I was thinking of taking out another one, if that's okay?" David asks politely.

Alice tilts her head in a slight bit of confusion. "You're returning a book?"

"Yes, the last one I just took out; it's due to be back today," David replies.

"Hmm, which one was it again?" Alice asks.

David sighs, "It's only been a week, did you really forget? It's the one with all the abyss notes and stories from other divers."

"Oh, right, that one; I've been too busy cleaning up to remember who took what book recently," Alice replies.

"I can tell; also, aren't I like one of six people who take a book out of here every now and then?" David comments.

"Seven, you are one of seven, thank you very much," Alice says as she crosses her arms in joking anger.

David blankly stares at her; his expression says all he would need to say.

"Well, I thought it was funny; anyway, hand me the book," Alice comments, as she extends a hand for David to give her the book. Grabbing it, she leans down, placing it on a shelf below the desk as she continues talking with David. "So, what did you think about taking out this time?"

"Hmm, I'm not sure, that book was the only one that had any information about the abyss, so it's not like I can get anything else relevant to it," David replies as he thinks, looking around to all the other shelves that line this place.

"Well, take a look around; I know you will find something interesting," Alice says as she stands back up behind the desk.

"Yeah, I know. If I find something, I'll let you know," David replies as he walks past the desk into to the maze of bookshelves.

Towering over David, these half empty to fully packed bookshelves can feel overwhelming at first. Choosing one aisle to walk down, David looks the books over; his gaze goes up, then down, then back up. One book catches his eye; he pulls it out—nothing more than a simple red book. Skimming it over, he learns that it's just a simple adventure story; David quickly places it back on the shelf, continuing his hunt. The sound of wind quietly whispers through the various cracks and holes all around the building. Looking through one shelf, David notices he is facing the front again. Between a few scarce shelves, David can perfectly see the front desk. Standing there, Alice is filing paperwork, placing it in a drawer, picking up a book, and making a note—just the small simple duties of her job. Yet, David finds himself stuck in place, just simply staring.

David soon groans out a little, thudding his head against the shelf. He whispers out to himself, "Say something, weather, no it's always terrible. My plans on going to the abyss; awful that'll just worry her. Work? No, who wants to talk about that? Compliment her looks; no, that might come off weird."

In the midst of David's anguish, a book falls out from the top shelf, smacking David square in the back of the head. He lets out a quick "Ow." As he picks up the book, he can hear Alice letting out her own giggle. Peering through the bookshelves, David notices that Alice has heard the commotion and was looking his way. The two notice each other, then look away, resuming their minor activities. Standing up, David sighs, placing the book back onto the shelf.

"You had a chance now; it's gone; good work," David mumbles to himself, looking for a new book once again.

Eventually, the day has gone on long enough; David cannot bring himself to make a conscious decision on what book to take out. Deciding to go with the simple route, David randomly selects a book from a shelf, then heads over to Alice at the desk.

"Hey, I would like to take this one out, Alice," David says as he places the book onto the desk.

"Hm, okay, then just let me make a note in here, and how long you want to take it out for?" Alice asks.

"A week, I guess," David quickly replies.

"Good, all done," Alice hands David the book. "I hope you enjoy it," Alice continues.

"Thanks, you too; your work, I mean, enjoy your work," David says as awkwardness fills his face.

Alice laughs slightly as she waves David goodbye. David stiffly walks back to the door before huffing to himself, then turns around. Approaching the desk again, David, in a more shy tone, speaks up, "I forgot I-I wanted to say, you look, erm, your dress looks nice today."

Alice's slight laughter pauses. She looks away, avoiding the conversation for a moment, fixes her glasses, then looks back at David. "Thanks, I patched the holes myself."

"Me too; on my own clothes, I did these patches too; anyway, I'll see you around." David straightens up and quickly makes his way to the door.

Alice's smile fills her whole face as she yells out, "Bye, I'll see you later."

Walking down the street, David fixes his eyes to the ground once again, mumbling to himself, "Dress! What dress! She's wearing overalls and a shirt."

David hurries home to read his mystery book. Entering, he greets his mother, who promptly asks if he feels alright. David asks what she means by this; his mother points out that his face is bright red. David quickly replies, "It's hot outside," avoiding any further questions, stating he wishes to read his new book. Going into his room, David sits on his bed; he checked out a new book, so he decides to at least try reading it. Opening it up, the first thing David is met with is a cartoonish drawing with only a small amount of letters at the bottom of the page. David has checked out a children's picture book. Seeing this revelation, David slams his head into the book and quietly whispers, "I can't show her my face ever again."

CHAPTER 7

THE LANDING

From a deep sleep, David is suddenly and violently woken up by Joseph who's standing over him with a smile from ear to ear.

"C'mon, get ready, we're going," Joseph says, eager to get the day started before the day itself has even started.

Rubbing his eyes, David asks tired and quietly, "What? Is it time already?" as the infamous morning bells have not even started yet.

"It's five thirty," Joseph says, while putting on his pair of rustic boots.

Still dazed and confused, David asks, "Why so early? Can't we wait a little bit? I'm tired."

Not taking no for an answer, Joseph, ready now, stands up, grabs David's blanket, and hurls it off of him. "We can't waste a single minute; after all we got a new job," Joseph says.

Groaning, David sits up and prepares himself for the day to come. As Joseph leaves the room, David looks around, taking in his room one more time. His bed broken and old but still comfy enough to get some sleep. The walls peeling with chips of paint, holes from age, wear, and tear, the floor barely holding the weight of itself up. Thinking to himself that perhaps this may be the last time they will sit in such an old worn out place, David thinks maybe they can move up in the housing blocks soon, getting away from all this. He's planning in his own head all the things he'd like to get to furnish a new home for the three of them and how nice it'd be to finally live in some sort of luxury, if only for a little bit. But dreams will have to wait right now. David has to tackle reality and keep moving on to make the dreams real. Bracing himself, he stands up, then heads straight to the bathroom first. After finishing his morning business, he heads to the large room where Joseph is waiting and their mother is still half asleep in her wheelchair.

David, looking at Joseph, whispers, "You didn't wake her to tell her what we're doing."

"We can tell her when we get back with all the money we'll make," Joseph replies softly.

Rolling his eyes, David quietly leaves the house, followed by Joseph. Full of excitement, quickly as the two can, they start to rush down to Mike's house to retrieve their belongings. As they come to a halt in front of the Mike's house, they see Mike is already waiting outside on the steps with all of their stuff.

"Hey, Mike, we're here," Joseph calls out.

Mike raises his hand, giving them a small wave as David and Joseph collect their gear. Looking over at them, Mike confirms with them about their gear. "Make sure your lamps are full of the oil you got; don't want your eyes going dark in there," Mike says.

Looking over their stuff, David and Joseph unscrew the top nob of the lamps, then begin pouring the oil into them. Filling the lamp to the brim, the oil cans finish dripping the last drops of oil out. They rush to screw the nob back on and attach it to the waist buckle on the backpack. Ready, the three of them set out to the dock; along the way, with the help of the growing sunlight, David takes a good look at Mike now.

He is standing at the same height as Joseph, just a little more lanky, wearing long hair tied in the back as it comes down to the middle of his shoulder into the center of his back. Mike's face is more sunken than Joseph's but similar in nature; at the bottom of his face, a short beard is starting to take root all around.

David's staring is eventually broken as they come to the same dock from last night that was sparsely populated but is now a host to more people than David could count. People crowd in all directions, moving from place to place, walking in groups, couples, or alone. Dock workers are unloading and loading docked steam ships, carrying boxes and goods to delivery trucks in waiting. Taking note, David even recognizes one truck; it's the same one that delivers the materials his factory unloads and sorts. David never really once stopped to think about where all that stuff he sorted day in and day out really came from. In the same thought, David never really thought where it goes either.

David looking out onto the water can see the steam ships in full motion going around to various ports on the island. Some ships are docking dropping off goods to another town, some ships are departing, a few of the large ones are going toward the gate, while some are on a trip back from the gate. Following all the commotion on the dock, David sees a long line of people with all the similar gear as them. He thinks to himself, That must be where the divers get to the gate. Joseph waves at David to follow them down.

"C'mon, Dave, the ship to the gate is over here," Joseph yells out.

With a small jog, David catches up to the pair just entering the back of the line. Down to the front, a woman stands asking for people's paperwork as they approach. At a small march, the line moves forward with everything working in sync. When one last person passes the woman, onto the docked ship.

"Boat three full!" a man by the ships yells out.

Noticing this over all the other commotion, David looks down over the side railing to the line of boats; they appear as simple as simple can get. On both sides of the boat, a steam engine is ready to turn a wheel of paddles half dipped into the water. There's nothing but four walls and one seat in the front where the operator of the boat sits. One wall face is flapped down, allowing the divers to board the ship quickly, then disembark just as quickly. When the boat is full, the wall retracts back up to complete the boat; easy and simple are all that's needed to describe these boats.

The line moves again after a brief stop; a new empty boat docks where the full one has left, ready and waiting for divers to board. Once again, the woman begins taking the papers, then writes something down on a clipboard in her hand. Step after step, the three make it to the front just before the woman; Mike in front hands Joseph two papers, then Joseph hands David his paper. A few more people in front of them proceed, then finally, first up to the woman is Mike.

"Papers?" the woman asks.

Mike hands the sheet to her; she marks it, then marks her clipboard. Second up is Joseph; the same thing follows. Joseph hands her the paper and once again she marks it, then marks the clipboard. Now it's David's turn; as he approaches the woman, she stops him, not asking for papers or saying anything.

"Boat four full!" the man from before yells out.

Concerned, David looks past her to Joseph at the foot of the boat's gate. Joseph shouts out to David, "It's okay, we'll meet on the island."

Without any concern, the boat gate rises up, and the boat, whole again, the ship departs. Waiting first in line now, David is alone; feelings of concern and fear begin to well up in his gut. Steeling himself, David breathes to calm down. I know it will be okay, it has to be okay, David thinks, calming himself. Soon, a new boat pulls into the dock and the gate slams down empty.

"Papers?" the woman asks.

David sheepishly hands the paper to her, who then directs him to the empty boat the first to board it.

David, standing against the back wall, looks down the boat as all the people are boarding. One after another, they walk on; first someone stands next to him, then the next person next to that person. Forming a row of people from side to side, packed shoulder to shoulder the people from another line in front of David. Standing in front of David now is a man of average size, slightly a head taller than David, gruff and worn out. As David stands, waiting in the early morning dark, the man turns around, looking down at him. The man seems to think to himself for a moment, then speaks to David.

"You a lucky one, huh!" the man says.

Confused, David responds back with, "Sorry?"

Rubbing his chin, covered with a slight five o'clock shadow, the man continues, "First one on the boat is a lucky one."

This still has not helped David clear his confusion; he asks the man to explain what he means.

"There's a legend for us older divers who go to the gate by boat every day. They say that whoever gets on the boat first is one to have luck inside the abyss. Something like that I think. I don't really care for dumb stories; just thought it's funny seeing someone so young."

Pondering to himself, David asks, "What of the last people on the boat?"

Quickly the man simply replies, "They're screwed." Shocked by his answer, David begins to worry for Joseph. The man continues, "I think it was something like that, or maybe it was the other way around."

David's distress grew after the first part of the legend but even more so now that the man is unsure which way the legend goes.

"'Course it's nothing more than a legend; I don't know many people who take it serious," the man finishes.

David tries to think nothing of the legend; however, deep down in David's gut, something feels as though what if there is truth to this legend.

David with no more time to worry about that, as the boat's gate begins lifting. Inside the walls of the boat, the turning of gears can be heard. The chains holding the boat's gate get pulled along the tracks on top of the walls, clinking away as they get reeled into a hole in the back just behind David. The gate shuts, the boat, together again, begins its departure.

Chugging along the open lake, the boat sways back and forth; a few people find it hard to keep their composure. Some people along the walls hold onto the walls to ensure they stay standing upright. The rocking of the boat intensifies; at times, the motion forces a handful of people to vomit inside the boat. The boat reaches the midpoint of the lake now; here, this being the furthest away from any land, the water becomes the roughest. Besides the crashing of the waves against the boat, not much else can be heard out here. All the bangs and clangs of the typical factory work have faded into the distance. For once in David's life, he gets as close as possible to complete silence. The only few noises inside the boat is a cough here and there, or someone sneezing somewhere on the boat. Small conversations between people break up the silence every now and then—talks of what they want to buy, what they will find in the abyss. Just past the halfway point, the sun begins to rise just beyond the hill of the island. The sky, being illuminated in deep purples and oranges, is streaking all across the sky in every direction. Slowly, all the colors begin to merge and fade away into a calm blue sky, finally giving the inside of the island light. The sunlight crawls along the slopes of the hill, making its way down to the towns and factories. Just as the light hits the water embankment of the lake, six o'clock rings out. For David, this feels alien for once, hearing nothing but the three loud bangs of a bell. The sun slowly passes over the boat, washing them in a warm light. As the boat inches closer to the island a specific painted green wooded pole juts out of the water, tall enough for David to see it over the high walls of the boat.

"Fifteen minutes, get ready!" the driver just above David shouts out to all on the boat. People begin collecting their items they had placed at their feet; some try and collect themselves, preparing to make the landing.

Slowing down, the boat comes to a crawl as the island begins to come into view now. David, behind everyone, tries his best to look over everyone standing all the way on the tips of his toes. Peering around and between the rows of people, he can see nothing but their backs and high walls of the boat. Suddenly, the boat jolts to a stop with the sound of sand being pushed from the hull of the boat; they have reached their destination. David can hear a click from behind, in the wall; suddenly, the chains begin racing down the wall as the gate is hurled to the ground. As the gate slams down, it comes back up just a little, then it falls, finally resting on the beach. Quickly, the people jog out of the boat onto a sandy beach; one row after another, the boat is emptied.

David, now at the lip of the boat's gate, can see the island in plain view for the very first time. Dotted all around further up the beach are rest tents in various configurations. Some are square or rounded, a few are large for multiple people, some just small enough for one person. Towering over all the tents, the gate into the abyss can be seen. Its massive size allows it to be seen from anywhere on this island, despite the various tents reaching into the sky. As of now, the gate is completely open, silent, like it's watching all the people below it go about their day.

David, not knowing what to do, simply follows the lead of some of the people who seem to know. While walking behind, David keeps scanning around for any sign of Joseph but so far to no avail. Suddenly the man David was following stops, with out warning David bumps into the man as the whole group has come to a stop. Organizing themselves the group stand in three different rows of people. David quietly stands in the back, blending in with the others as he observes what's goes on. Peering between the rows of people, he can just catch a glimpse of a large older man walking out of the large tent in front of them. Standing in front of the group, the older man looks them all up and down.

"Anyone who has been here before can go do whatever you want to do; just get out of here," the older man loudly proclaims.

The once large group has now thinned out to just a handful of people in a row, David now on the far end of it. David watches the old man, wondering what he is doing. The old man walks down the row of people; he eyes each person standing before him, scanning them, evaluating them, judging them. Finishing this, the old man rubs his gray beard and turns away from them.

"You will all die," the old man begins, then pauses briefly. He turns back to face them and continues, "And my job is to make sure that it is of old age." Pacing back and forth from the small line of people, the old man begins his rant to them. "The gate holds within it the abyss, and the abyss is death. I can train you and teach you to cheat death and come out with valuables in hand, at your discretion. Ultimately, your survival is up to you; I can only do so much for you. First off, I'm the gate commander. I oversee everything that happens here; I am a busy man. I organize all of you; I make sure all goods get to the correct ships; I also make sure your families get the letter notifying them of your death."

Someone raises a hand and interrupts the commander. "Shouldn't they get our bodies if we die?" the person asks.

"If you die in the abyss, there is no body to recover," the commander replies, then continues where he left off. "You will address me as gate commander or just commander. As of now, you all are a part of Gate Exploration Team 974." Pulling small patches from his pocket, the commander hands them to each of the people present. The commander begins again, "These patches are for organization purposes. Don't pay them any mind; they mean nothing more than that. Now the rundown of how everything works. You all have accepted the task of entering the abyss and pulling out from it anything of value." The commander pulls a small bar of iron from his pocket, then holds in one hand. From the other pocket, he pulls out a small bar of gold in the other hand. Holding them up in front of his face, he explains. "This is iron, plain and simple; we use it for construction or useful materials, and this is gold. Gold is used for expensive items, like jewelry and ornate pieces of art. Everything else is labeled an oddity; some oddities go for extremely high prices, some aren't worth the sand we're standing on. Noticing the difference is up to you; take it or leave it, that's your choice. Now, what is stopping you from taking all these items? That's where the darkness comes into play. We don't know what it is, we've never seen it, and frankly we probably don't want to. All we know is, if you let your light go out, it will snatch you up. The only thing that follows is a gruesome death. The few bodies we found after they died are twisted and bent in ways the human body should never go. Parts of your body may be torn out, ripped from your insides. Pray you don't find the bodies of those that get taken. Next is your time limit; as you all are aware, at six in the morning, the bells rings out; that's when the gate opens. Then at six at night, it repeats, but now the gate will close; but be wary, ten minutes before the gate closes, the fire starts. Again, we don't know where the fire really comes from or how it gets started, just the fact that it does. It starts all the way from the bottom of the abyss, then moves up; the fire starts and moves with no regard to your life or anything in its way. It will swallow you whole and leave nothing behind. So make sure you know when to start heading back up here, and never let your light die out." Scratching the back of his neck, thinking about everything he said until this point, suddenly the commander continues, "Oh, right; I got ahead of myself there." Pulling a small round object from his back pocket, he clicks a small button on the side. The small object opens up into two halves: the bottom half, a compass pointing off into the direction behind them; on the top half, a clock ticking away showing the current time, just a little past six thirty. Holding this small trinket up to show the people, the commander walks back and forth again, explaining, "This is your compass and clock; when this introduction is over, you will all get one. Remember that I said, if you break it, you will not get another one free. These are extremely expensive, and you have to buy your next one if this breaks. So what does it do? Well, for starters, the clock is self-explanatory; it's a clock. The compass is a bit different; this will always direct you to the gate, inside it or out of it. How it works, I don't know; I didn't make it, nor have I spent any time trying to find out how it works. Lastly, any questions?" Pausing briefly The commander looks down the line to wait for questions, at the end of the row David raises his hand. The commander looks at him and asks, "What is it?"

"Do we have to go in with a team or by ourselves?" David asks.

Thinking to himself once again, the commander replies, "I guess I forgot that part. Teams are not a mandatory thing; you can go in it either way you want. Both have pros and cons to them. A team will allow you to get more support but at the same time more hands to take any loot you might find. On the other hand, going solo allows you the privilege of getting all the loot to yourself but less support. So weigh the difference yourself and decide for yourself." Pausing, the commander waits to see if anyone has any questions.

Again David raises his hand and asks, "What do we navigate through down there?"

The gate commander, interested, swiftly begins, "Well, you're a curious one; you will encounter doors to go through that may lead to a room or a staircase that goes down. In these rooms, you will find the loot, and if you find a staircase, you can descend a floor. The further down you go on the floors, the more the loot becomes abundant and valuable. So search the rooms to the best of your ability and find your way down if you want more value out of a dive. Is that all for the questions?" The commander pauses, waiting for another question that never comes, then resumes, "Then head into the tent, pick up your compass, exit the other side, and get moving into the gate."

Leading the way, the gate commander turns around and enters the tent first, followed by the line of people. David, last into the tent, comes to a table where the commander is sitting. The commander leans down and reaches into a box beside him and pulls out a compass and hands it to the person standing at the table. Then the next person walks forward and then the next person, until lastly David stands before him. The commander pulls out what will be David's compass; as he begins handing it to David, he stops and looks up at him.

"Are you related to a Joseph Stich?" the commander asks.

David shakes his head up and down and replies, "Yes, he's my older brother."

Nodding, the commander says, "Thought so; you look like a smaller version of him; he was in the boat just before yours." Then the commander hands over the compass to David.

As David leaves the tent, he can hear the commander wishing him good luck. Pulling the tent door flap out of the way, he sees, just a few tent rows down now stands the "Gate," the center piece of the island. Before running off, David places the compass into his pocket, then begins looking out for any sign of Joseph and where he might be.

CHAPTER 8

FIRST DIVE

Walking toward the center of the island, David passes empty tents, tents with people resting, and tents of people fixing their equipment. With the gate just in front of him now, David can faintly hear Joseph speaking. Coming closer to the large gate, David gets this sense of being minuscule as he stands in front of this structure. David looks at the gate from top to bottom, then notices Joseph and his friend Mike hanging out and talking to one another. Approaching, David greets them and waves them down to notice him. The pair quickly notice David and greet him, joking about how it took him much longer to get here. Joseph, being eager to enter for the first time, asks them if they are ready to finally enter. Checking all of his gear, David confirms that he is ready, along with Mike who does the same.

Joseph is the first to step foot through the gate into the abyss. The temperature suddenly drops, the air in here is cold and still. The stone floor, along with the wall, are deeply charred. Despite the sun shining outside, Joseph looks down the hallway and cannot see a single thing. He turns his lantern on; even with this aid, he cannot see any further than before. It's as if the air itself is eating any light cast on it. Fully stepped in now, Joseph turns to Mike and David; as Joseph looks at them, he shrugs, suggesting it's time for them to come in. Mike takes a moment to look down at David, before turning his own lantern on, then entering the gate. David takes one more look at the opening. His heart beats faster than it has ever before, so much so he thinks it might come out of his chest. Despite this, David finds the courage, turns his oil lamp on, and pushes himself into the abyss. Quickly, David hurries to Joseph's side as the three begin their first dive into the abyss.

As they walk down the long corridor, it gets darker and darker; soon nothing but their oil lamps are the only light to be seen. David, curious, pulls the compass out of his pocket and notices the needle pointing straight back behind them. Reassured that it's working before he puts it away, he takes a mental note of the time: 7:04. Suddenly, David crashes into the back of Joseph who's standing still. David puts away the compass and peers between Joseph and Mike to see what has made them stop. In front of them are five doors; they appear as black as the darkness around them—burned and charred metal, held together by rivets on the right side; jutting out at waist height on the left side is a small U-shaped handle.

Simultaneously, Joseph and Mike ask, "What is this?"

David sighs, "Didn't either of you ask what was down here?"

"I think that old guy explained something, but I didn't feel like paying attention; just wanted to get to the gate," Mike replies.

"I was pretty distracted by how much larger the gate was this close," Joseph says.

"Fine, I'll explain then; the way we move through the abyss is through doors and rooms; a door will go to a room or a staircase, simple," David says.

Joseph and Mike shake their heads, agreeing.

"Anyway, of the five doors here, only one has not been opened, so I guess that's where we have to go," David says pointing to the closed door.

The three look at one another and silently decide who should be the first to go. Mike steps forward, the brave one to open the door. As Mike opens it, he pokes his head through, then looks from side to side and then steps through. David and Joseph stare at each another one more time, then Joseph steps through, followed by David. Standing on the other side of the open door, the three look around. There is no staircase so they must be in a room; surrounded by complete darkness, they cannot see anything of note. The three decide to keep walking forward into the room. They agree to split up and look around for another door or any treasure, and if they find a staircase, they are to wait for the other two. Mike proceeds forward deeper into the room while Joseph goes left, leaving David to go right. Walking along, accompanied only by darkness now and his lamp, David begins his first search.

Emerging from the darkness at the tip of David's light, a square metal bar stands straight up. Getting closer to illuminate more of it, David finds the bar continues upwards above his head and stops. At shoulder height, another bar stretches out to the left, then another bar stretches away from him. In between the outer bars, there are smaller bars going side to side, connecting them. David holds up his lantern, illuminating the whole thing now; he finds the bars come together to form multiple squares. Horizontal thin metal bars connect a square by his feet and the one at his shoulders.

David, thinking out loud to himself, says, "Well, it's too large to carry, not to mention, rusted, but what even is it? Kind of looks like two beds of metal with lots of holes in it. Can't be great to sleep on; might as well continue looking."

David begins walking once again to only find more of the strange metal formations neatly put into rows. Passing so many, David lost count of how many he has passed. Suddenly to his left, David hears a loud banging and crashing noise. Hesitant to investigate, David wonders what that could have been. However, out of concern for his brother, he decides to check on it. Creeping closer to the sound of the noise, David discovers Mike sitting on the ground, the metal bars collapsed like a cage on him now.

"Mike? What are you doing?" David asks.

"I thought I could sit on it for a minute; next thing I know, the whole thing crashes down on me," Mike replies.

Pulling the metal away from Mike, David sets him free. Just as he is regaining his composure and dusting himself off, Joseph shows up. Joseph also came to investigate the commotion. Together again after a short time, they decide that not much can be found on the floor; in fact, none of them have found anything. They check the time; it has only been thirty minutes: 7:34. Knowing they still have all day, they decide to look for the staircase to the next floor in hopes to find something to bring back. Within minutes, the three of them have finally found another door—7:46. Opening the ominous door, they step through once again, braving the darkness. Going forward together, they come to what feels like the same room. In the same neat rows sit the metal structures again. Confused, the three pull out their compasses, confirming that the needle is pointing the way they came from; nothing has differed. Although confused, they walk again, to find the door this time with more haste than the last time. Opening this door, they hope to find something other than the same room again, and to their surprise, it is a staircase.

As they look down the staircase, they can only see the first five steps and nothing else. David and Joseph look over to Mike standing next to them.

"What? I went first last time; one of you go first this time," Mike blurts out.

Now David and Joseph look at each other, then Joseph speaks up, "Well, I'm the older one, so I guess I'll go first this time, but, Dave, you're going next time."

"Fine," David says as he shakes his head, agreeing.

Ready as much as he can, Joseph takes the first step down, pauses, takes a deep breath, then continues walking, followed by David, then Mike. The previous door has vanished into the darkness as they continue descending. Soon, they reach the bottom of the stairs; a small square land-ing just like the one at David's home appears out of the darkness. At the edge of the landing, attached to it, is a door. Opening the door, Joseph steps into another dark room, walks forward, and comes to once again the same metal structures as the last floor.

"What?" Joseph says loudly.

Confused, the three look around; nothing has been changed from the last floor.

"Do you think the abyss is broken?" Mike asks.

David and Joseph only look at Mike blankly and refuse to humor his question.

"What? It could be a possibility," Mike says.

Turning back around, the three of them continue to look around for anything that could be changed or different. They all asked themselves the same thing: what if something is going on; their only choices are to either figure it out or leave. Passing one row of metal structure, they all come to another row; this one, however, comes with large chests at the foot of the structures now. Each large chest has the same appearance as the doors, black as the darkness and charred looking. Holding them together are straps running vertical, evenly spaced out and held on by rivets. The chest is quite wide, wide enough to fit an entire person into it, if need be. The three of them look side to side, nothing but the same repeating chests to their left and right. Joseph and Mike look down at David and motion him to open the first chest and look inside.

Sneaking up to the chest, David puts his hand onto the handle of the top hatch. Without any resistance, it opens; the top of the large chest swings upwards on its squeaky rusty hinges. Keeping just one eye open, David looks inside for anything dangerous. As the top half of the chest comes to a stop, David realizes there is no danger; as he opens his other eye, he finds nothing more than a clump of iron scrap. This scrap is just like the one the gate commander held before. Picking it up off the base of the chest, the three look at their first piece of treasure. Silently, they look at each other, then back at the scrap. Soon, Joseph and Mike go in separate directions to open chest after chest and pulling out its contents and stuffing them into their backpacks. David gently puts the iron scrap into his backpack, then takes a glance at the time, just to feel a bit of comfort: 8:12. Having the whole day to go, David goes his own way forward to find more chests as well to open them and find more of his own treasure.

Coming to one specific chest, David looks side to side but cannot see any other chests. This one stands alone. Just as before, David opens it; to his surprise, unlike before, this chest appears to have no bottom. Pulling his lamp from his waist, David holds it next to his face as he kneels down, looking into the chest, trying to illuminate the inside but to no avail. Light cannot reach the bottom of this chest for some reason. Concerned, David puts his lamp back on his waist. He takes one look at the clock from his pocket and quickly notes the time: 8:48. Now, as David starts to stand up from the chest, suddenly at that moment, a thick black tendril whips out, wraps around David's neck, and yanks him into the chest. The chest lid promptly falls closed.

David's feet are no longer on the ground; he flails both his arms and legs any way he can but still cannot feel any surface. David has this feeling of being suspended in the air; he no longer knows which way is down and which way is up. Nothing is being illuminated except for the tendril stretched out from the darkness clinging to David's neck. Fear consumes David as the tendril coils tighter around his neck, suffocating him; then it loosens for it to adjust, giving David a brief moment to breathe. Soon, another tendril comes from the left, grabbing David's wrist; fighting it with all his strength, David tries to pull his hand away. However, his struggle is in vain; his arm is now straight out to his side. More tendrils come for his right arm, then both his legs. David, now strung up like a freshly caught animal, is spun form left to right. Flipped and turned, David loses what little sense of direction he had before. Suddenly, from the darkness, a disembodied voice speaks up; it's tone deep and guttural; it hangs on each word and speaks slow. It sounds as if multiple people are speaking from one voice.

"This one pure of heart. Strong. Heart made of stone and light," the voice groans out.

The tendril around David's neck curls up to his face, turning his head from side to side; the voice continues, "You cannot be a vessel. You are not broken. But. You are needed. You will aid my fire and brimstone. Rejoice. You shall act as another cog."

Just as fast as David had appeared in this space, he has been expelled out of it. He is forced backwards. The lid of the chest flings open, and he is ejected from the chest, his back crashing into the inside of the chest lid. Bouncing off the lid, David is deflected onto the ground. Quickly, the chest lid closes once again on its own volition. Laying on the floor, David holds himself in pain. Taking a moment to catch his breath, he tries to understand everything that just happened. As the pain subsides, David opens his eyes, realizing he is back at the foot of the chest. Confused, David takes out his clock; opening it displays the current time: 10:48. Shocked, David quickly sits up, looking closer at the clock. He even rubs his eyes, thinking something is wrong. David jiggles it to see if it is working correctly; he even slightly taps it with his hand. He then glances down at the needle; it steadily points off to the left; at least one thing works like normal. Looking around, David can neither see nor hear anything else around him. Concerned that he has no other option, he slowly inches closer and closer to the chest. Thinking this may be a horrible idea, he creaks the chest lid open. David slowly raises his head over the opening, revealing a normal chest inside. Bottom and four walls, nothing missing or strange. However, resting right in the middle is a shining gold nugget, the size of David's palm. He looks around, thinking this could be some elaborate trap. First David pokes the walls, then the bottom. Nothing happens; safe and sound, David picks up the gold with both hands. Raising it up into the air, David inspects it, rotates it, insuring there is nothing going on. After a few minutes of looking at a piece of metal, David decides nothing is wrong with it. Perhaps, he thinks, he fell asleep and everything was a dream, or some hallucination. David places the gold into his backpack; standing up, he regains his bearing and senses.

Walking out of the darkness behind David comes Joseph calling out to him.

"Oh! Dave, I finally found you; this floor must be huge," Joseph says.

Turning around, David sees that it is, in fact, Joseph. Still a bit scared from his experience, David questions Joseph.

"Joseph, what time is it?" David asks.

"Like, uhh," Joseph pulls out his clock to look. "10:52, why, don't you have a clock, or did you already lose it?" Joseph says.

Looking around in confusion, David thinks for a minute. "Did anything weird happen to you, Joseph, or in general at all?" David asks.

"No, nothing besides looking for you for the past hour. What happened? You fell asleep or something?" Joseph asks.

"No, well, at least I don't think so, maybe I did, I'm not sure at this point," David replies.

"Well, I for one think it's a little early to start going crazy. So how about you take a moment and calm down, okay?" Joseph says.

Heeding his advice, David takes a moment to calm himself. In this moment, David also decides to keep everything that happened a secret for the time being. However, he will become more cautious of anything that happens from now on. Once more, Joseph speaks up.

"Me and Mike have filled our bags and have decided to go for some food; it's probably best if you come along too," Joseph says.

"Yeah, that's a good idea," David replies.

The two begin to follow the needle on the compass to leave. Coming to the door with the stairs, they find Mike waiting. During Joseph's search, it appears Mike had fallen asleep. Joseph sighs, then kicks Mike's foot, waking him up. Reunited, Mike greets the two; they all get ready to leave. All together now, they proceed up the stairs and back through the same two rooms they had gone through before. As the needle changes, the group follows where the needle tells them. Soon, the needle has brought them right back to the beginning, the entrance of the gate. Their first ever dive into the abyss is complete with both loot and their lives.

CHAPTER 9

NEW EXPERIENCES

E merging out of the darkness, David, Joseph, and Mike have gotten their first ever taste of the abyss. They begin to look where to drop off their acquired loot. Joseph notices, just to the left of them, a table with a man sitting behind it. On both sides and even behind the man, heavily armed men stand, clad in black metal-plated armor around their chests, legs, and arms. They hold in one hand a pike; as the blunt end sits on the ground, the sharp end easily raises above their heads. Sheathed at their waist is a sword, similar in size to the one Joseph bought. Resting on the table is a balance scale, both sides empty as it awaits for something to be placed on it. Joseph is the first to decide to go over to the man, followed by David, then Mike. Approaching the man, he waves to them.

"Come to turn in some treasure for money?" the man greets them.

Simultaneously, the three agree; Mike, the first one to unpack all that he had found, places each object on the table—nothing more than some scrap pieces of iron with an occasional piece of silver. Peering at each piece and studying them one by one, the man rests it on one side of the scale. After all the metal has been placed on the scale, it teeters slightly on one side. The man pulls out a bag from below the table; as he places it on the opposite side of the scale, it makes a jingle sound of coins slashing together. Slowly, the scale levels out but not all the way to perfect. The man reaches down again, pulling up loose coins; he places one coin at a time, until the scale is perfect. Finally, the scale steadies itself, then the man pulls out a small notepad. He begins writing on it, then from a small safe under the table, withdraws a stack of paper money. The man flops the money on the table and announces to Mike.

"Four hundred and fifty-six dollars," the man says.

Nodding, Mike picks up the money, safely places it in his pocket, then steps out of the way for Joseph to step to the table. Joseph begins unloading his backpack onto the table. The man clears off the scale and drops all the metal into a box next to him. As the box has been filled to the brim, the man claps once, and a worker emerges from the tent. Following the worker is another guard; the worker comes over, picks up the box, then walks back into the tent with it. The guard places an empty box next to the man where the last one sat, then returns to the tent. Repeating the weighing process, the man inspects Joseph's belongings. Once again, the man reaches down, taking out the money for Joseph.

"Five hundred and five dollars," the man says.

Lastly, David walks up to the table. He looks into his mostly empty backpack with only a handful of loot. He pulls out the few pieces of scrap he has, then at the end, pulls out the shining gold nugget. Everyone's eyes widen a little bit; the guards break composure for only a second, giving small glances at the gold. As David places it on the table, Mike and Joseph stare at him.

"What?" David says, full of discomfort from all the staring.

Snapping out of the daze, Joseph pats David on his back and smiles, "Nice job; with your skill, we'll be rolling in money in no time," Joseph says.

Letting a small smile escape, David rolls his eyes, turning back to the man who had already set everything on the scale. Unlike Mike and Joseph, David's belongings seem to tip the scale far more significantly. Surprised, the man pulls out another bag of coins, placing it on top of the previous bag. The scale is still unsatisfied; the man places more coins on top of the two existing bags. Finally, the scale is satisfied as it sits perfectly levelled. Humming to himself, the man at the desk nods, looking the scale up and down furiously and writing in his notepad. When the man finally settles down, he struggles to bend down, reaching deeper into the safe. Standing up, the man clasps in both hands a large quantity of money.

"Three thousand six hundred and fifty-seven dollars," the man says.

David, Joseph, and Mike can only blankly stare at the large amount of money on the table, quietly blinking in astonishment. Looking back at each other, David and Joseph share the same thought. In one morning, David has single-handedly made three times the amount of money the two of them made in a week. Coming back to reality, David picks up his earnings, puts a sum into his pockets, but having no more room, he has to stuff the rest into his backpack. Before they turn to leave, Joseph asks the man sitting down, if there is any place to get lunch on the island. Pointing off into the distance, he directs them to a tent, the largest at the camp, assuring them that it's the cafeteria where they can find all kinds of food and drinks. It can also be a temporary place to rest if they have not set up their own place to rest on the island yet. Departing off, the three wave to the man and thank him for the trade.

Strolling through the camp, the group watch all the goings-on: people who have just arrived on the island, people getting ready to go dive, and other people getting out of a dive. Eventually, the three of them end up at the large open tent lined with rows of tables and chairs. People are all about, sitting, standing, ordering food, eating food; the cafeteria is quite a busy place. Scouting out the tables, Mike points them to an open table they could sit at. Walking over, they sit down, getting some time to finally rest and have a moment to decompress. After a few minutes pass by, Joseph stands up excitedly, arms wide open, and shouts to David and Mike.

"Lunch is on me; I'll get us all some food," Joseph says.

With a spring in his step, Joseph enters the end of the food line at the other end of the cafeteria and waits. Mike, looking on, chuckles a little; he begins to rub the nape of his neck to let some stress out.

"What happened down there, by the way?" Mike asks David.

Exploding with concern, David looks over at Mike; David can feel the blood rushing out of his face.

"W-what do you mean?" David replies awkwardly.

Sighing, Mike asks again, "What happened? Joseph couldn't find you in that room for almost two hours."

David's eyes dart from side to side, attempting to avoid eye contact and trying to come up with an answer. "I-I don't know; I must have been just missing you guys," David says.

Peering at David, Mike says, "Me and Joe kept bumping into each other the whole time for the first hour and not you; that's a little weird."

Attempting to end this as fast as possible, David continues to stall. "I don't know what to say; the abyss is a weird place," David says.

"Yeah, we gathered that, but where did you go?" Mike asks.

"Nowhere I swear; it's just weird, that's all," David replies.

"Hm, I know, we only just met, so you don't have to tell me anything, but Joe is your brother; don't hide anything from him," Mike says.

"Yeah, but, I don't know. Would anything change if I said something?" David says, looking down at his hands in his lap.

"So, something did happen. So, why can't you tell us, or at least Joe?" Mike asks.

"Because, it's just this feeling; it doesn't matter if I say anything; nothing will change. Even if we wanted to change whatever happens, I don't think we can," David replies.

Just before Mike can question David once again, Joseph appears, setting down three plates of food on the table, interrupting them. Full of astonishment, Joseph tells them of all the food they have here, pointing to their plates. Mike and David compose themselves, then stare down at the full plates of food, wondering what half of it actually is. None of them have ever left their housing district. They never had the money to buy any kind of food that was more than what they could afford. Looking it all over ,David points to a sliced piece of white meat.

"Joseph, what is that?" David asks.

"The food lady called it turkey. It's a bird of some kind," Joseph replies.

"Like the birds at the dock?" Mike asks.

"Or the birds that are always on top of our house?" David asks.

"No, it's some large kind of bird we were never able to see," Joseph replies.

Nodding, David and Mike look down at the plate full of food in bewilderment. Mike picks up a round shaved like object.

"And, what is this called?" Mike asks.

"Mike, that's just a potato; don't you ever cook?" Joseph replies.

"No, well, nothing more than whatever scraps I get from the store. Anyway, is the food supposed to be this green?" Mike says.

"The only green food we had was moldy bread," David replies to Mike.

Joseph stabs the long thin green plant, then holds it up. "We can't buy many vegetables, but these are string beans," Joseph says.

Leaning toward Joseph's fork with the string bean, Mike asks, "Why is it called that? Does it have string in it?"

Joseph swats Mike away, "No it doesn't actually have string in it; it just sort of looks like string," Joseph says.

Mike sits back in his chair. "Ahh, so you going to eat your green string not-string beans."

Joseph looks at Mike, then at David; it appears Joseph has been put into a position of going first. In his excitement, Joseph never asked if any of the food was good. However, it cannot be any worse than the food they have been eating before now, could it? Quickly, Joseph shoves the fork full of string beans into his mouth. At first, confusion fills Joseph's face; as he continues chewing, he silently thinks.

"Hey, this is pretty fantastic; you guys have to eat something now," Joseph says, after swallowing the string beans.

One after another, Joseph stuffs forkfuls of string beans into his mouth, then moves on to trying everything else sitting on his plate. David and Mike take one moment to look at each other, then down at their plates and back up. They decide it's best to just eat. All three plates full of food, none of them ever had a chance of trying until now. Turkey, string beans, broccoli, slices of ham, black beans, chicken—every bite of food, a new experience. Once the plates are empty, the three feel as though they have eaten more food in this one sitting than in their entire lives. Sitting there, they all lean back, satisfied for once with their stomachs full of food.

"I could pass out right now," Mike says.

With one eye already closed, Joseph agrees; however, David affirms them that they have to keep watch over their money. As he looks over, he sees it's too late; Joseph and Mike have passed out. Sighing, David finds the strength to sit up, stretching a little bit. He looks over to the food counters, the line never stops. For brief moment, David sits back, thinking about how great it would be to share this food with his mother. However, he knows he cannot. If he had brought back such great food, the fact that they went into the abyss would be exposed to her. With the other two asleep, David being bored takes in the sights, sounds, and the people. Other thoughts, like where and how to save all his money, come to mind as he sits here passing the time.

After a brief hour has passed, Joseph and Mike wake up from their nap. David, still awake, jokingly wishes them good morning. From here, the three try and plan out what they will do for the rest of the day. Ultimately, they decide to head back home for the day and prepare to leave. Collecting their belongings and leaving the cafeteria, they walk back through the camp once again. As they walk, David notices the gate commander standing alone in a sunny spot, reading over some papers. At this moment, David thinks to himself, then tells Joseph and Mike to go on without him for the moment. Building up some courage, David walks up to the commander. Noticing David approach, the gate commander folds up his paper and places them in his pocket and greets the young boy.

"You need something, kid?" the gate commander starts off asking.

Looking up, David replies "I thought of a few more questions after my first dive this morning."

"Good, you survived; that's a start. And knowledge is a valuable tool, so ask away," the Commander says, nodding.

"When I first got here, you said you can train us to not die in there. Can that training help you to not get caught by whatever is in there?" David asks.

"Hm, sounds like you ran into something; anything you feel like sharing?" the Commander replies.

"No, it's nothing, just, you said you could train us but never actually trained us, so I'm curious what that training is," David replies.

Rubbing his chin, the commander answers, "That's more or less a speech I give to all the new people. The important part of it is, that everything is up to you. Diving is a choice we all have; I stopped because I got old. So I put that age of experience to good use, like being the commander. I am in no way responsible for what happens to anyone who dives; I just manage everything for the organization's sake. If you have the dedication, I can train you to help better your odds like I did," the Commander says.

Pondering what the commander had said, David tries to keep it in the back of his mind, then asks. "What kind of training is it then, anyway?"

The commander is taken aback a little as he was never actually asked to train anyone before. No one ever asked. Thinking back, the commander pulls out a rag from his back pocket, then asks David to turn around. David cannot come up with a reason to say no, so he complies and turns around. The moment David turns, everything goes black. The commander puts the rag over David's eyes, then ties the back of the rag. Leaning down to be right next to David's ear, the commander explains.

"We rely on our eyes to see everything. Which works well as long as we have light to see everything. The only problem is, in the abyss, you have no light, so you have to learn to see without your eyes."

"What? How, and that doesn't make any sense," David says, confused.

"That's what I'm going to show you." For a moment, the commander pauses, then begins again. "You need to listen and feel what's around you. Listen to sounds; everything makes one, even the wind. Listen to the direction, the intensity, listen and see without your eyes. It'll take time to do it correctly but keep trying. With everything going on in the camp, try to pinpoint the different sounds. Envision them, measure the distance by volume, feel how the air changes from the slight vibrations."

David peers intently into the darkness, thinking, waiting, feeling but nothing comes to his sight, just empty blackness. Sighing, David tells the commander nothing is happening and how it is not working. Swiftly, the commander chops the top of David's head with his hand.

"Don't ever give up. If I'm going to train you, then I will not tolerate giving up. I told you this was going to be hard and will take time. Did you expect to be a millionaire on your first dive too? Come out with enough money to buy the world or something?" the commander yells.

Rubbing the top of his head, David responds, "No."

"What was that?" the commander asks.

"No! I'm not giving up," David yells.

"Good," the commander replies. "You'll get better at this, so long as you keep pushing; oh, and also try to bulk up a little; you're too scrawny to lift much down there."

"Uh, how do I do that? I've never worked out before," David replies.

Under his gray beard and mustache, the commander has a devilish smirk; he says, "Glad you asked."

David is still blindfolded but is now lying in the dirt, with face down and hands pressed against the ground right next to his chest, attempting push-ups. Standing over him, the gate commander counts as David slowly pushes up one more time.

"Twenty-three!" the Commander says.

As encouraging as the commander can be, he reassures that after fifty push-ups, David will do crunches, then squats, and finally a run after this. David, once again face in the ground, wonders why and how he got himself doing all of this right now.

"This will make me better; this will make me better!" the Commander yells out over and over. "Keep repeating that in your head and keep pushing."

Slowly, David completes the push-ups, then lies completely flat on the ground, out of breath and sweating. With his foot, the commander hooks into David's stomach, rolling him onto his back, ordering him to begin his crunches. Taking one last deep breath, David does everything he can to hoist himself up, then back down, continuing his crunches. With the blindfold on, time has become hard for David to decipher; as of now, it felt he had been working out for hours. He finishes his crunches, taking a moment to breathe lying on his back. With one arm, the commander grabs David's shirt from the center, hoisting David back onto his feet, having him begin his squats. Shaking like a leaf, David stands there, squatting halfway.

"Lower, lower, I said, lower," the commander yells out, making David's knees come to a ninety-degree angle.

David pushes his legs into the ground, using everything he has to stand back up. Getting slower and more lethargic, he stops to stand for a brief moment, bringing his face to the sky to get some deep breaths in. All over his face and forehead, he can feel the sun between the trails of sweat. After taking in the sun, David wipes off his face a little bit, then dips down, continuing his workout. Finally coming to an end David hears The commander count to fifty. David falls to one knee, resting for just one minute.

Clapping his hands together, the commander excitedly tells David, "Ha-ha, now the running can begin."

"Why?" David asks, tired and confused.

"Because, you asked to be trained, so, get up," the commander says.

"Okay, but what about the blindfold? How can I run like this?" David says, pointing to his face.

"Follow me. Hear the weight of my feet on the ground and my running cadence," the commander replies.

"Ca-what?" David asks.

"My running song," the commander replies.

"Oh, no. Well, what if I hit something or run into someone?" David says.

Grinning at David, the commander simply says, "Don't."

Turning away now, the commander begins to jog, telling David to follow his voice and feet. Sighing, as if he had given up all reason, David attempts to run into the direction he hears the commander. Immediately, he runs into the pole of a tent, his legs give out on him, and he falls to the ground. From a distance behind him, he can hear the commander.

"Ha, you've gone the wrong way, kid; I'm over here!" the commander yells.

Gritting his teeth together, David stands back up and grunts as he runs into the new direction. David's training goes on for some time; he runs to where he thinks the commander is, to only find out that it was wrong. One last time, as David runs, something clicks in his brain, something has made him hear more clearly. David listens as he runs toward the commander once again; stopping, he pauses. The sound of the footsteps from the camp residents are all around like they have been, the whole time. However, now, to David, a certain pattern of footsteps stand out among the rest. David himself doesn't know why or how, but these feel different; he focuses on them. He listens to them, one heavy foot in front of the other. David begins following them, seeing them in the darkness under the blindfold. The mocking tone of the commander dies out; now, the only sound that remains are these footsteps. Running, David follows after these footsteps; he follows them step after step, stepping wherever they step. After a short while, David begins running out of breath, his sides hurting, his legs shaking more than before. Just as he thinks he is about to fall, the footsteps disappear. Without any time to process this change, with full force, David crashes into a wooden crate. Lying on the floor, he rubs his nose and slips off the blindfold. Crouching down on top of the crate, laughing to himself is the commander. Following with a small clapping, the commander bursts out.

"Oh, you started to get the hang of it there, huh? That's good progress, but you can't tunnel vision it. You have to learn to take everything in," the commander says.

Confused, David looks down at the ground, then around him, and finally looks up at the commander and asks, "What just happened?"

"It's simple; you followed me jogging, you listened to the sounds, and saw without your eyes, all be it for a brief moment," the commander says.

Thinking back to just a minute ago, David comes to the conclusion; he did it.

"That was really weird; I was seeing things but not seeing anything," David says.

Crawling off the crate, the commander explains, "It is a weird feeling; you'll get used to it. Our brains are powerful, powerful enough to create what's going on around us with such limited information, like hearing. Learn to keep seeing by listening and you'll have no problem getting through the abyss. Well, that concludes our training for today. Feel free to come see me when you think you want more difficult exercises or to work out together again. Other than that, I trust you'll keep working out yourself, right?"

"Yes, I will. Also can I keep the blindfold," David asks, nodding.

Smiling, the commander looks down at David. "Sure. Well, then, congratulations!" the commander says as he walks back off to do his work.

After taking a moment to collect himself, David stands up, dusts off his clothes and backpack as best he can, then finds his way back to the beach.

Walking out onto the beach, David finds one boat empty and waiting. Standing just in front, Joseph is waiting for David to arrive. As Joseph waves to David, he looks him over and asks what happened. Sighing a little, David explains.

"I ran into the commander and we did some work outs," David says.

"Remind me not to run into the commander ever," Mike says from the boat.

Shrugging his shoulders, Joseph just accepts it, then the two walk onto the boat. Coming to the back of the boat where Mike is sitting on the floor, Mike looks up at David, laughing a little about how dirty he is. David decides to take a seat next to Mike on the ground as he continues to try and catch his breath, trying to relax. David looks up at the sky the sun just slightly past the center of the sky as midday has slowly passed by.

Over David's head, the ship driver asks, "Was he the one they were waiting for?"

"Yes, we can leave now," Joseph replies. As the driver nods, he turns around beginning the ship operations. The door lifts up, the engines roar to life, and the boat sets off for home.

CHAPTER 10

SMALL TREASURE

The boat rocks back and forth as the water crashes against the outer walls. As the port comes into view now, the engines shut off; they begin to slow down to a stop. Gently, the boat drifts into place beside the wooden dock that's jutting out from the land. With a deep thud, the boat finds its resting place, coming to a full stop. Lastly, the door comes down, landing on the dock face, making a bridge between the boat and the dock. Like slugs, David, Joseph, and Mike trod off of the boat, back onto land, then up the ramp into the dockyard, back to familiarity. With clear blue sky above them and the sun just past noon, they decide to head back to Mike's home to rest and unload their gear, until it's time to go home. Before they could leave, however, David and Joseph hear familiar voices calling to them. Running over to them, a group of people they know from work in the factory come to greet the two. The small group crowd around them and berate them with all kinds of questions.

"Where did you guys go?" one person asks.

"What did you guys do?" another person asks.

"Did you really go into the abyss?" someone from the back asks.

"What was it like in there? You find anything interesting?" More and more questions come at them.

Trying to quell them, Joseph tries to answer all of them as much as possible, half answering and half boasting their feat. Pushing his way through the crowd, a young boy falls out from between two people. Noticing the familiar stature and clothing, David excitedly greets the boy.

"Sean! What are you doing?" David says.

Fixing his hat, Sean stands up, then looks over to David. "Shouldn't I ask ya that?" Sean replies. Taking a moment to breathe in, Sean continues "Me and some boys from work were down here taking lunch. Next thing we notice, you three walk off the boat from the island. What are ya doing on that boat anyway? Ya really went into the abyss, ya a diver now?" Sean asks.

Rubbing the back of his neck embarrassingly, David answers, "We sort of did become divers."

Sean's eyes widen with excitement after hearing David answer him; practically hopping up and down, Sean has even more questions, "What was it like? What did ya do? Did ya get a lot of money?"

Overwhelmed by the continuous question after question, David tries to calm Sean down so he can answer them. Looking around the crowd, David finds a path out of the crowd; pulling Sean with him over to the side, he lets out a deep exhale.

"Finally, we can breathe a little," David says.

Just as quick as the peace had come, it is gone. Sean once again beats David with questions, and once again David tries to calm Sean down. "I know you're excited, but can you give me a moment here, Sean? I just got back and I'm pretty beat," David groans.

"Sorry, sorry, it's just so cool, knowing a friend went to the abyss," Sean replies.

The pair look for a spot to talk, over by one of the building out of the way from the middle of the dock, but still in view of the group. David takes a moment, leaning up against the wall, resting, while he answers Sean's questions.

"Okay, okay, so what do you want to know first?" David asks.

"Well, first, what was the island like?" Sean asks.

For the next few minutes, David finds the strength to answer every question Sean has. However, he remembers to leave out the encounter he had; other than that one tiny detail, he tells Sean everything.

Suddenly, a distinct whistle shouts all across the dock, interrupting David's conversation. Sean glances over at a clock in the street, realizing lunch has come to an end.

"Damn, we gotta get back to work, huh! Well, I'll just steal your ear later for more questions," Sean says

"You still have more questions?" David says, rolling his eyes.

Laughing with a wide grin, Sean waves goodbye to David as he walks off to the group. Joseph finally pries himself from the crowd of people and walks over to David waiting by the building.

"Hey, you ready to head back to Mike's house?" Joseph asks.

David nods. "I'm looking forward to lying down for a bit."

Laughing a small bit, Joseph pats David on his shoulder. "Well, when we get this kind of money, we'll be able to lie down whenever we want to," Joseph says.

Smirking, David replies, "Yeah, yeah, you mean when you get that money; for now, this is mine."

Joseph laughs. "Don't worry; soon I'll get that kind of money too," he says.

"Yo, found you guys; what's the deal, leaving me to fend for myself in that mosh pit." Mike says as he approaches David and Joseph.

"Hey, you need to be able to take care of yourself, Mike; I'm not your mom," Joseph says.

"Anyway, are you guys ready or not? I'm still tired here," David says.

Getting back on their path, the three leave the dock area, continuing their way to Mike's house. Upon getting to the front door of the house, David looks off to the side, telling Joseph and Mike he wants to go do something first. Joseph and Mike nod, waving David off as they enter the house. David walks through the alleyways, making his way to an open road with the sign over a large gate reading, Shopping District 16. Entering the open road, David is greeted by one half of the road's buildings selling pitiful amounts of food. Scraps of fish, steaks, molding bread, all the way to rotten vegetables. Just across the food stores, various store fronts sell a wide range of items—broken home goods, such as cracked plates, rusty silverware, cups all chipped and riddled with holes. One store sells beat up furniture, chairs with three legs, sofas ripped and torn, mattresses with springs poking through. Another store sells toys and knick-knacks, held together by the bare minimum of material. Here, in one of the lowest shopping districts, there is nothing to brag about; nothing is considered second-hand at this point, more like fifth hand by the time it falls here. However, this is all David has to work with, so he shall work with it; as he peers past broken windows into what you could call a shop, he walks up and down the street. One woman, dressed in rags, sitting on a stool in front of one shop, calls to David.

"You look like you want something; what is it?" the old woman says in her crackly voice.

A little surprised, David answers. "I'm looking for a small storage chest with a lock, you know, something to put stuff into."

"I know what a storage chest is; come in here," the woman retorts. She flings her arm out to David. "Help an old woman up and I'll see what I got inside," she says.

Shrugging, David decides to help the woman up, who then in turn leads him into the hobbled-together store. The rotten old wooden door creaks open as the two walk in. Hung above the door, a small rusty bells only chimes once as the door closes. Looking around, David takes in the surprising amount of stuff in here; although most of it is junk, the amount is impressive to David regardless. All kinds of things hang both from the ceiling and on the walls; on the floor, cabinets make a maze of the whole store. Littered on the shelves of the cabinets, are toys, silverware, picture frames, little jewelry boxes, and much more, all covered in dust. While trailing behind the old woman, without looking behind her, she begins talking to David.

"So what size box are you looking for?" the old woman asks.

Tilting his head slightly, David thinks for a moment, trying to envision how big of a box he would need. Something small like a jewelry box would be too small and something like a storage trunk would be too large.

"I guess something of medium size, still small enough to be carried, but large enough to hold a lot of stuff inside," David says.

As the old woman thinks, she scratches just behind her ear, then comes to a halt. "A-ha, I think I have just the thing for you, little one," she says.

The old woman shuffles one foot in front of the other, slowly moving across the store. She comes to a wide cabinet, nearly twice the size of the hunched-over old woman, then swings open the doors of the cabinet. From behind, all David can see is the old woman shoving object from side to side, humming as she looks at one object and tosses it to the side. Her mumbling slowly fades away.

"Ha, found it," the old woman shouts, surprised.

As she turns around, in both hands, she holds a metal box. Just a little wider than both of her hands and only one hand length deep; she presents the box to David for his inspection. David gently takes the box from the old woman, turning it around, upside down, then undoes the latch, opening the top, looking inside the old box. While David is still investigating the box, the old woman begins talking.

"I believe, workers call this a toolbox; it's quite sturdy despite its age; its spacious and can be carried. Also it's the only one I have of this size, so I think it's perfect for whatever you need," the old woman says.

David, interested in the box, asks, "So, then how much will it cost?"

"Just ten dollars," the old woman says.

Thinking it over, David decides that it's a decent price to pay for the box, so he agrees. He pulls out his money from his pocket, handing the paper bills to the old woman. New box in hand, David leaves the store to go on his way.

As the wind blows, that old familiar taste in the air of an impending storm in the sea approaches the island. Climbing the old cobblestone steps now, David passes the tops of the buildings, coming to his old faithful tree on the edge of the island. Under one arm, David's newly acquired box was held firmly against his ribs and forearm. For a moment, David takes in the sight of the ocean, as he always feels compelled to do so whenever he is up here. Only a week has passed; while the sun may be hot, the wind carries a brisk cold chill with it up here. The cold air reminds David that his time is going to run out faster than what he may hope for. His estimation is, three months and three weeks are left, at best, for his mother. Opening the box, David places two thousand dollars into it, keeping the rest for necessities and other expenses.

"Two thousand down, nine hundred and ninety-eight thousand more to go," David whispers to himself, looking into the mostly empty box.

Closing the lid of the box, David kneels down; using both hands, he digs a small hole at the base of the tree. The hole is just big enough for the box to fit into; David lays it down to rest, pushing the dirt over it for safe keeping. Wiping the sweat from his forehead, he stands back up.

"There now, my small treasure can be safe. No one comes up here anyway; it's where the grass grows," David whispers as he looks toward the island. He watches the hustle and bustle of everyone's lives as the sun falls closer to the horizon.

CHAPTER 11
STRANGE FOREST

Three weeks have passed from David's very first dive; two months remain before his mother's disease fully takes hold of her. The world as a whole has not changed; the island moves as it has always done so. Little bits of change has come to David, however, and his small family. Their quality of life has improved greatly since they started a new job as they've said. Money became stable, food was no longer rotten all the time, clothes fit and matched. However, a new concern blossomed inside David; after every dive, he would roughly save most of the money he earned, in his box. Along the way, Joseph had also donated to help, of course. Recently, however, Joseph stopped saving money.

As the boat sways side to side, the waves crash against the outer hull and the sun begins its morning routine of rising to the sky. David and Joseph stand side by side, waiting for their morning travel to be over. During these three weeks, David has continued his training to make himself stronger. Along with the intake of more food, David has surprisingly grown a little.

"You're starting to fill in a shirt, Dave," Joseph says, smiling, looking down at David. Then he makes a fake a crying noise, "They grow up so fast."

David, embarrassed by Joseph, joke slaps his back. "C'mon, stop, it's just all the training I'm doing. I keep telling you to do it with me too," David says.

"Please, diving gives me all the training I need to get through everything," Joseph says, smirking.

"Well, when I have to drag your lifeless body out of the abyss again, I'll remind you of this very moment," David quips.

"Hey! That was one time, and I was knocked out so it was not entirely my fault," Joseph quickly replies.

David stands there, shrugging his shoulders and shaking his head. Interrupting their joking together, the man operating the boat yells out that they will arrive on the island in a few minutes. Joseph picks up his large, more expensive backpack and gear.

"Well, you ready to get to work today?" Joseph asks, looking at David.

David does one last check of his gear to ensure everything is correct, David replies. "Yup."

As the boat's rocking slows down and the engines dies down, the boat tilts up as it lands on the shore, coming to a halt.

Walking off the boat and then up the beach, David looks down and notices new people arriving as well to the island. The new people begin forming the lines in front of the big tent as instructed; the commander walks out to greet them as he does all the others. Loudly, the commander begins his speech, chewing the ears off of all the new divers.

Nudging David's shoulder, Joseph points over to them. "Ha, remember that it was only three weeks, but it feels like it was so long ago," Joseph says.

David laughs a little to himself as they keep walking into the camp to find Mike at the tent he has set up. While walking through the camp, a few people greet the pair of brothers as they make their way around. Some people wave to them, others silently nod to them, and someone even calls out to them.

"You know, it feels weird, having some kind of renown around here," Joseph remarks to David.

"Well, surprisingly, not many families enter the abyss together, and it seems that the few that did, ended up breaking apart." David replies.

"Ooh, spooky," Joseph silently whispers.

"Nothing exciting like some kind of legend; just either they die in the abyss, or they just stopped coming to dives all together," David says.

Standing tall, puffing his chest out a little, Joseph says, "Well, I'll still keep a vigilant eye on my back for safety."

Waving his hands David brushes Joseph away, David scolds him. "I think I'm the one who has to watch your back."

Quickly, Joseph slumps a little, "Hey, that's kind of mean."

David jokingly smiles as the two continue walking. Soon they make their way to the tent bought by Mike. Coming up to the fabric acting as the doors to the tent, Joseph enters first, finding Mike still asleep on the cot. Sighing, Joseph lightly kicks the cot's frame, holding it off the ground, shaking it and waking Mike up. Rubbing his eyes in a tired state, Mike rolls over.

"Just five more minutes, yeah," Mike murmurs.

Letting out a long deep breath, Joseph sighs again, then yells out, "We're going to be left behind if you sleep all day; the team's waiting for us," Joseph slaps Mike on the face.

Quickly, Mike jolts up. "I'm awake, I'm awake," he yells out, while rubbing the palm print on his face now.

"Good, then get ready; we'll be outside, waiting," Joseph says with a smirk, walking out of the tent.

Emerging from the tent, yawning, Mike steps out, still dazed and tired but awake. Just like Joseph, Mike now dawns on more expensive gear than they had started with; diving is paying off good for them all. Together now, the three depart to the gate. As they arrive to the gate, a small group of four other people are standing around, looking at their clocks. The one man in the middle takes notice of the three approaching and greeting them.

"Well, look who decided to show up," the man says. This man stands just a few inches taller of Joseph. Despite his younger appearance, the man still appears to be the oldest of the group. Thick stubble is attached to his lower face, only a small handful of wrinkles line his eye. His short thin hair stands up on all ends. Standing in front of them, his size and build are average.

"Hey, guys, Mike was still asleep again," Joseph says as he raises a hand to wave at them.

The young girl steps forward, rubbing her brow in frustration. "Well, that figures as much." Standing before them at most, she is only two years older than David, and her height is just shy of David's. This makes her the smallest in the group. Her brown hair runs past her shoulders in a ponytail.

"Rest is important, Sam." From behind the whole group, a large tall man towering over everyone else there, speaks up in a low tone, addressing the girl. The man is easily a head taller than anyone there. His larger frame demands more space as well, making him appear more intimidating than he is. His face is soft and cleanly shaven; just as his jaw lacks hair so does the top of his head.

Crossing her arms, Sam speaks, filled with a bit of frustration. "I know, Ben, I know, BUT we still have a time limit here to keep."

The man at the end of the group speaks up, "Well, if you want to talk about wasting time, aren't we doing that right now instead of, you know, going in?" This man is similar to Mike in appearance, however, surprisingly more lanky and skinny. Just on his upper lip is a thick mustache. Unlike Mike, this man is also bald rather than having long hair.

As the group turns, they look over at the man who just spoke; as they turn back away, they all agree to continue on into the abyss.

The first man who greeted David's group walks by the man who made the suggestion, patting him on the back. "Hey, good job keeping everyone moving, Henry; that's real surprising coming from you."

Henry laughs a little. "Well, I would like to make some money today, Ant."

The group all together now, take a final minute to check their gear one last time. Being overprepared is never a bad thing in the abyss. The group check their own gear and even turn to each other to check someone else's gear. Final checks done, the group make their way into the gate, proceeding into the abyss for just another dive.

Stepping through the darkness, the one acting as a leader, Anthony approaches the first set of doors; this time, there are ten of them. Three of the doors are open; the rest are closed, turning this into a group vote. Anthony turns to face the group in the darkness.

"So we got seven doors to choose, any suggestions?" Anthony asks.

David, Joseph, and Mike agree that whatever Anthony chooses will be fine.

"Whichever door smells more like money to you, Ant," Henry says.

Sam looks over and points out the second door from the right. "I'm feeling, that one."

Ben stands there in silent agreement of what the group decides.

"Well, Sam, guess we go with your gut; hope it's a good one," Anthony says to the whole group.

"Probably not," Sam replies.

Creaking open the door, Anthony steps through into a room full of nothing but rows of empty metal shelves. As the group enters, they each inspect one of the solitary standing shelving units, some of them hold small valuables, others nothing. Overall, they decide to find the way to the next level down. The first to find a new door is David; upon opening it, he comes to a room containing nothing but rows of empty chairs. Henry comes over, finding David at the open door.

"So what'd you find, little buddy?" Henry asks.

"Seems to be a dead room; I don't think there's anything worth it in here, Henry," David replies.

Curious, Henry enters anyway, stating, "Well, the way down could be here anyway; might as well take a look."

Taking a moment to think, David agrees, then begins searching the room for another way. As David and Henry are searching the room, they pass by rows after rows of chairs—neatly organized, perfectly positioned, nothing more nothing less, just chairs. Henry is most disappointed that there is not a single instance of any treasure to be found. David walks up and down the rows; looking off into the distance, the chairs are facing as well. David even takes a minute to sit on one chair; sitting there, he stares into the empty nothingness. One question passes David's mind, Why? Why so many chairs, all facing the same direction? What does it all mean? Does it mean anything at all? Everyday, questions like these fill David's mind dive after dive. As he stands back up to continue his search, images flash in his mind briefly. Images of a crowd of people sitting in the chairs, facing the same direction. Clapping, cheering, celebrating, for something, for someone. Just as these images came, soon they are gone. David stands there looking around side to side, peering down each row, then looking back forward, in the direction the chairs face.

David begins walking through the rows of chairs in the direction they all face, breaking the neat organization of rows. After a short walk, David finds a door leading to a staircase. He meets back with Henry, telling him he has found the stairs down. As Henry waits at the top of the stairs, David goes back to the previous room, gathering everyone to proceed down. Now that everyone has gathered at the staircase, Anthony leads the group down with Henry directly behind, excited at what is to be found next.

Coming to the bottom of the stairs, another door awaits them. Anthony carefully opens the door; to the group's surprise, it's another set of stairs leading down. They all look at each other briefly, knowing this is a strange situation but regardless they decide to walk down the next set of stairs. While walking, Henry airs some of his thoughts to the group.

"So, do you guys think this puts us on the fast track to getting more money?" Henry comments.

"Who knows if that may be true, but this whole situation feels a bit weird," Anthony replies.

"To be honest, Ant, it's the abyss; everything is a bit weird. We seem to just find something a bit weirder than everyone else," Mike speaks up from the back.

"I think we'll do just fine; we get to a room, collect some fancy rare stuff, and leave; a simple one, two, three," Henry says.

Still concerned, Anthony tells them all to be vigilant and to take note of anything that happens. Coming to the bottom of the stairs now, a new door awaits; slowly, Anthony opens the door but stops midway as he peeks through it. His eyes widen full of surprise and bewilderment, his face loses all color as he stares through the door.

Excited, Henry steps forward. "What's the holdup, man? Let's go," Henry says as he walks through the door.

Just as one foot of Henry's enters the door, Anthony screams out, "HENRY! WAIT!"

Anthony was too late to warn Henry; quickly, he follows him through the door. Surprised, the rest of the group decide to file into the door, following Anthony. Upon entering the door, the whole group stops in dumbfounded surprise as to what is set before them.

Bright blue open sky, dotted with pure white clouds, trees as high as buildings and as round as a person. Vines creep and jump from one tree to the next, forming long ropes. Vibrant green vegetation covers every piece of dirt on the ground. The land goes on for what appears forever in every direction. The oddly strange thing that stands out now is the solitary door that the group has come through, standing out in such vibrant green plant life. Filling their ears are the sounds of birds, small insects, and creatures, moving and living about. The leaves high above their heads sway from side to side as they get pushed by the wind. Rays of sunlight shift and move as the leaves create different and new gaps for the sunlight to break through. Breaking up everyone's astonishment, Joseph speaks up.

"Are we still in the abyss?" Joseph quietly asks.

Only Sam manages to reply, "I have no idea." Looking over to Anthony, Sam continues. "Hey, Anthony, you ever heard of this?"

Anthony, still looking up and around, just quietly replies, "No, I don't think anyone has ever seen this."

"Okay, well, I don't think anyone has any idea what's going on obviously, but do not turn off your lamps. I know it seems we're outside and it's strangely daytime and light out, but I believe we are still in the abyss. So we should be fine if we keep our lamps on regardless," David says, addressing the whole group.

Henry scoffs a little. "What makes you so sure about that?" Henry asks as he reaches for his lamp. "I ain't burning oil for no reason." With that, Henry turns off his lamp.

As soon as his lamp is off, one of the vines quickly whips down from one of the trees above, wrapping itself around Henry's neck, pulling him up and cutting off all oxygen. The group gasps in surprise, but just as quick as the vine has come down, Joseph runs to Henry's side, drawing out his sword and slashing the vine in half. As Henry falls back to the ground, he pulls off the severed vine from his neck. As the vine falls to the floor, it loses its green color, turning to a deep black char, then breaking apart to ash. Joseph quickly turns back on Henry's oil lamp for him and Henry collects himself. After gasping for some air, he thanks Joseph multiple times.

"It's no problem, Henry, but it seems Dave is right; we're still very much in danger," Joseph replies as he puts his sword back.

Lost in his thoughts, David comments, "Strangely so, we seem to be in the abyss but it's unlike anything in the abyss anyone has seen or encountered."

The group becomes even more confused by what David has said, each of them coming up with their own questions that no one can answer.

Joseph steps forward and asks, "What do you mean by that, Dave?"

David continues his thought, "Well, first off, obviously our surroundings; no one here has heard any such story of this happening. Second, Henry was almost immediately killed. Every and any story about anyone losing their lamp light was instantly dragged away and killed horribly. However, despite all those two reasons, the compass is still working fine, but it seems the clock has slowed down almost to a stop." David holds up his clock to show everyone the second hand coming to a crawl as it moves. He continues, "So, now the surmounting question that we all have is, what is going on?" As David finishes his explanation, the strange time occurrence takes him back to his first dive. His fear grows, of what might happen or what might be controlling all of this.

Anthony, collecting his thoughts, asks, "So, faced with this, we entered this place at about 10:23, according to our clocks. But let's say at a normal rate of time, we still have a few hours to explore this place and get out safely. What does everyone else think?"

"Well, if we can find anything of value here, then I'm all for it." Henry is the first to speak up.

Sam, Joseph, and Mike agree with Henry's thought.

Ben quietly replies, "As long as we stay safe."

David agrees with Ben.

With the group all in agreement, Anthony announces, "All right, we'll stay safe and find something of value. However, it seems that normal diving rules still apply, so keep that in mind plus some extras now; we shouldn't interact with any other life. Or eat anything," Anthony specifically points to Henry.

"Hey!" Henry yells back.

Standing more confident now, Anthony checks on the group. "Everyone ready?" Looking around, Henry stands back up as everyone gathers themselves. "Okay, let's go," Anthony says, leading the group into the forest.

Marching through the forest, Anthony pushes and shoves all kinds of leaves, bushes, and overgrowth out of the way, carving a path through the thick jungle. Eventually, they make their way to a stretch of dirt that runs from their left to right, as if someone had made a path. Stopping, Anthony thinks for a moment.

"Normally, I'd say let's split up and go both ways, but this situation is not normal," Anthony says.

Mike comes forward. "Is there anything of note on the ground or anywhere else, like some kind of marker maybe?"

They all begin scanning the dirt pathway, trying to decide which way would be best. Soon, David shouts out to the group.

"Does anyone recognize this?" David asks.

The whole group gathers around what David has found. Looking down in the dirt, everyone in the group tilts their heads in thought.

"This looks like some kind of imprint. It's in the ground but I don't know what it looks like," Joseph says.

Sam pushes her way forward to get a better look. "It's got a big odd round spot and five smaller ones and . . ." Sam pauses as she leans closer to look at it. ". . . some lines coming from them." Sam stretches her arm out, placing her hand into the center of the imprint; her entire hand fits inside of it.

"Man, this gets weirder and weirder. You think it's worth anything?" Henry asks.

Putting his hand on Henry's shoulder, Ben looks down at him with concern. "Henry, it's a patch of dirt."

Looking up, Henry wears an annoyed face at Ben's comment.

Anthony steps forward. "Anyway, it could be some kind of marker, so let's follow the lines in the direction that it seems to be going."

Leaning over, Joseph asks, "How do you know that?

"I don't; let's go," Anthony replies and begins walking down the path.

As the group begin walking down the trail, David stays behind crouched down with his face in a small book. Joseph notices David still behind; concerned the group might lose David, Joseph calls out to him to hurry.

"I'm just finishing drawing this symbol," David replies.

David then closes his notebook and puts it away, then catches up to the back of the group.

"Why did you bring that little notebook anyway?" Joseph asks.

"I think it would be a good idea to write all the stuff we see down here, like some kind of diary. Or, at the very least, some kind of journal for other divers in the future," David replies.

"So, what do you have in there anyway? Not much has happened lately, and let's be honest, Dave. The stuff we seem to experience, I don't think will help anyone else," Joseph says.

"Yeah, I know right now I don't have much, but who knows what we'll find, and who knows, maybe one day, someone will follow our footsteps," David replies.

"Ha, I hope no one goes through what we are right now," Joseph says.

As they walk down the forest trail, the sound of rushing water starts to come into range; as of now, it's soft and far into the distance. Soon the sound of water grows louder and louder, becoming deafening, drowning out any other small noise. Eventually, Anthony, at the front of the group, finds himself overlooking a large circular chasm, all the way at the bottom, a type of shallow lake. Just on the other end of this hole, across the group, a river flows off the edge, creating a waterfall.

As the group stands admiring the view of the water flowing down into the lake, a crack of thunder is heard just above their heads. In an instant, above the middle of the chasm, a ring of golden light appears right in midair. Suddenly, what appears to be a man, falls, his screaming muffled by the waterfall as he rushes toward the bottom of the chasm. The group in stunned into silence as they see a man appear out of nothing and watch him as he falls. The man is too far off for any detail of his character to be visible. Just as quickly as he appeared, the same hole appears below in the middle of the lake, swallowing the man before he was about to hit the rushing water at the bottom.

Stunned, only Sam speaks up, "What was that?"

No one else could come up with words to describe what they all saw. Blinking a few times, Anthony pulls himself back to the reality of where they are. He turns around to the group.

"Well, besides that, these same symbols from before go down this path to the left. The path seems to go to the bottom of the hole; perhaps, we'll find something of value down there," Anthony shouts.

Patting Anthony on the back, Henry passes him and takes the lead, "I like that attitude."

"What!" Anthony replies, over the noise of the waterfall.

Unable to hear each other, Henry gives Anthony a thumbs up, then proceeds down the path, followed by the rest of the group. To everyone's surprise, the deafening sound of the waterfall gets more quiet as they descend. Just past halfway down the trail, the noise is almost non-existent. Coming to the bottom and looking around, the group notice the lake exits into a tunnel in the wall and just climb down. Around the edge of the lake there's a small beach to walk on. Looking around, Henry notices another hole in the wall, just behind the waterfall.

"It seems the water shoots off the wall at the top and lands away from the path into the lake. I say, we go on in over there and find some treasure," Henry says, pointing the tunnel behind the waterfall.

"I don't know; seems rude not to knock," Ben comments.

"It'll be fine; we can just apologize to them; let's go!" Henry says.

The group make their way over to the hole behind the waterfall; from their original distance, the hole seemed much more human-sized, but now up close, it has nearly doubled in size. Standing at the secret opening, the group observe the hole in the wall. The height is more than what a person needs to stand up, the rest of this empty head room only comes off as excessive. The width is just as wide as the height; if something is in here, it is quite large.

Anthony looks over to Henry. "Still going to apologize to them now?"

"Oh, please, the gate is much larger than this dirt hole; c'mon in, it looks cozy," Henry replies, in his attempt to brush off Anthony's comment.

As they walk down the long, dark damp burrow, the sunlight fades away and a new small dim light appears in the darkness, one on both sides of the walls. Upon closer inspection, they notice the light is a small flame levitating in the air in front of a strange circle with even stranger symbols. Again, David decides to pull out his small book to scribble down the symbols for reference. As the group walks, more and more of these flames appear, lighting up the tunnel as the group comes to the dead end. Now, in front of them, at the dead end, the group can notice a small bookshelf off to the side, littered with scrolls of paper and books. Directly in the middle, there's a table; however, only the left and right side are visible. Obstructing the middle of the table, along with another light from the table, there's a large round-shaped object. It appears to be round as well as covered in brown hair from top to bottom. The group come to a halt just only a handful of steps away from this thing. As the group stops, the round object begins to move and shift. All the way to the top, it starts to elongate in size, going from a ball to a tower. Slowly, the topmost part begins to rotate and come into view—it's a face, a face of a beast of some sorts. The light on the table flickers to show more detail. The beast has large brown eyes; below them, part of its face juts out; on the tip is a small black nose. As the beast locks eyes with the group, its nose lets out a quick deep huff. Now the whole body turns to face the group; its massive body straightens upright and its head nearly touches the roof.

Anthony looks over to Henry, holding onto his back. "Well, go on, apologize to that," Anthony says, with fear in his voice.

The moment Anthony finishes his sentence, the creature opens what can only be a mouth, letting out a loud intimidating roar!

When the rumbling of the walls subside, Sam screams out, "Run!"

Together in unison, the group quickly turn around, making their way to leave the cave. They sprint as fast as their legs can move, rushing so fast out of the cave that Sam and David almost run straight into the waterfall. Rounding the corner of the cave, the group stop outside on the beach, halfway to the ramp back up. Catching their breath, Joseph turns back to the tunnel entrance. The creature is coming out of the cave; it turns, looking directly at the group.

"Hurry, it's coming after us!" Joseph yells.

Once again, it roars, startling the group into motion, to begin running up the ramp. Cresting the top of the path back to the ridge of the chasm, the group make it back to the forest. Anthony, the last one up, looks back, the creature just getting to the bottom of the ramp still pursuing them. With the loud crashing of the waterfall, Anthony can only push the group and wave to them to keep running away. As the group run back down the path they came, the sound of the waterfall is lost in the distance. Finally, as they run, they can hear themselves again.

Out of breath, Sam asks, "So what do we do now?"

"I say, we get out," Anthony replies.

Joseph pulls out his sword, then turns to David. "Lead me to the door; I'll cut anything in the way."

Nodding, David stands right behind Joseph and pulls out his compass to begin directing Joseph where to go. As Joseph listens to David directing him where to go, the group sprint past trees, through bushes, leaping over felled trees and large rocks. Joseph carves a path through the thick growth, listening to David telling him where and how much to turn. Finally, after running for what felt like an eternity, the door makes its appearance; they are almost there, almost home. Joseph, the first to reach the door, stands next to it, letting David in first. After David, Henry jumps in, then Sam, Mike, Ben, and finally Anthony. Before entering, Joseph looks back into the forest one last time and hears the thumping of the beasts running. Far off in the distance, Joseph for one last moment, meets eye to eye with the beast as it comes to a halt beside a tree. As the beast stops, Joseph wastes no more time looking and turns around, entering the door.

The group is now lying at the base of the stairs; half of them are on the stairs, attempting to catch their breath. Back in the darkness, the only thing heard for this short moment is all of them panting and huffing out of breath. Trying to get as much oxygen back as they can, David, however, notices that he is the first one back on his feet. For a moment, David looks around, noticing that the door has actually closed behind them. Before investigating the door, David looks at his clock first: 10:24. David's clock is moving at its normal speed again; he is perplexed as what felt like hours, was only one whole minute. Putting his clock away for now, David decides to open the door once more, only to peek in on the other side. Upon creaking it open, he finds nothing but empty blackness, a normal room; the forest was gone.

As he enters the new room that's appeared, David notices that unlike all the other rooms, this one is quite small. A simple few steps to either side would illuminate the wall; however, along these walls, David has failed to find a door. Even stranger still, seven chests sit in the middle of the room. These chests are simple in design and function; a simple latch holds the top lid closed. Observing one chest, David cannot find anything of note; they are simple chests, nothing more. Now that everyone has rested, they notice David has entered the room and decide to walk in as well. Noticing the chests, Henry is the first to choose a chest haphazardly, and he begins to open it.

"What are you doing? We should find out what is happening here," David swiftly says.

"It's the abyss; we're not going to find out what happened, and there are seven chests and seven of us, so it all works out," Henry says as he scoffs David's idea.

The rest of the group look at each other, then agree to go to a chest of their choosing. Henry, being the first to open his chest, finds in it an ornate gold necklace, adorned with red gem inlays. Joseph, the second to open a chest, finds a sword in a decorative black and gold sheath; when he draws the sword from it, it shines like gold with a sharp edge like no other. He looks at his old, dented beat-up sword and decides to walk over to David, handing him his old sword.

"Here, I know you never really thought about having one. But I'd rather you have it than let the sword go to waste in some trash heap," Joseph says, holding the sword outstretched in his hand against David's chest.

"Thanks, Joseph," David says as he attaches the sword to his belt.

Next, Sam opens her chest; David notices she pulls out a plain red book, its only detail, a small gold flower inlaid at the top left corner. Sam opens it, then skims a few pages before quickly placing it into her backpack. Ben opens his chest now to find a large new jacket; this new one replaces his old jacket that felt restricting on his larger frame. The jacket fits like a second skin, a perfect match. Inside Mike's chest, he finds three bars of gold; picking them up, he murmurs slightly.

"Hmm, thought there'd be more," he softly says as he puts the bars away.

Being the last two, Anthony offers David to go first; however, David insists Anthony go first. Anthony thankfully accepts. Inside his chest, Anthony finds a smaller box, just larger than his hand; he opens it, then quickly shuts it, just as fast as he opened it. With it being so dark, David didn't get a good glimpse of anything and thought to ask what it was, however, thinking it'd rude to be nosey if Anthony doesn't want to tell, David ultimately decided not to ask. Finally, David opens the last chest; with a heart filled of anticipation, he cracks the top open and pushes it up out of the way. Sitting inside the chest, David finds, nothing.

"Wait, what?" that's all David can let out, being at a loss for words.

Everyone else takes a peek inside to see if perhaps there might have been something in there but to no avail; there's nothing, just an empty box. Coming up behind David, Joseph pats David's back.

"Well, sometimes you just don't get anything; that's the way it is here," Joseph says.

The group apologizes for David's slight misfortune; however, David affirms them they did nothing wrong; the abyss is just simply cruel, and unusual.

With one of the strangest encounters the group has had in the abyss, they decide to leave for the day. The spoils they gained are enough for most of the group to be happy. However, as they leave, Anthony and Sam share a quiet look with each other, as if they understand they need to talk about something. As they leave the abyss, the only one to hand in their treasure is Henry. The others decide it best to keep what they have found. David notices Sam and Anthony walk off, their faces slightly concerned. He tells Joseph he will go and talk with them and leaves. As David catches up to the pair, he asks them if anything is wrong; concerned, David offers any help he could give. The two try to brush it off, but David can tell they are acting strange and hiding something. David presses the matter more, telling them that he understands the feeling of not wanting to talk about certain experiences. The two clearly want to confide in him but don't know if they can yet. Thinking Sam and Anthony will not open up, David tells them to follow him, away from any groups of people.

Together now, the three secretly hide between groups of empty tents. Confident that they are alone, David begins telling them what happened on his first dive. He takes this moment to be the one to open up first. David tells them everything, down to the smallest detail. In the end, Sam and Anthony stand shocked and hold onto some disbelief in the beginning. However, with the conviction that David tells his story and with such detail, it convinces them that he's telling the truth. Now that they know this is not David's first time experiencing something strange like this, the two begin opening up. Sam decides to go first.

"I don't know how to start this really, but I'll have to try. First off, you know that book I got; it isn't just some random book; it's not empty too. It's my diary from when I was little; my parents bought it for me as a birthday gift. I wrote everything in it. How I felt that day, what I did, what I saw, everything; I treasured it dearly. One day, I was writing as I sat by the sea, thinking how pretty it all looked. The coast is very windy if you've been there; that day, a strong wind came through. As I covered my face, my diary was swept away from my hand, and it fell down the cliff into the ocean." Sam chuckles a little as she crosses her arms. "I cried for days when I lost it; nothing my parents did helped me; buying new ones never replace what you had. As you age, you sort of move on, but never fully, it seems," Sam looks down at the book longingly.

After a minute, Anthony begins, "So this makes everything stranger then. My box held papers in it; important papers to me at least." Anthony opens the box and holds up one paper. "The box holds my adoption papers from when I was young. My birth parents abandoned me at an orphanage, where I grew up most of infant years. One day, my adoptive parents came in and chose me; to be honest, I was a pain to them in the beginning.

Once you get so easily abandoned, it's hard to accept others. But as I grew, they continued to love me regardless of all the problems I caused them, and eventually, I felt like I had a family and a home. To me, these papers solidified that family, like a symbol of who I was and who saved me, so I kept them in this exact box. However, one day, our home caught on fire; I couldn't save the papers. Just like what Sam said, as I grew I tried to move on, but that hole in your heart will always remain. So now, the question is, why and how did these things appear in the abyss, perfectly intact?"

For a moment, they try and think of a possible reason for all of this to happen. David speaks his idea.

"This is only a guess, but it seems the abyss or that thing in it gave us what we want. I mean, it gave us what we really wanted or truly desired. It's hard to explain, but it just feels like all the things we wanted really. Whether it be superficial or something personal, it gave us something we wanted," David says.

After David finishes, Anthony speaks up, "I can see where you're coming from. But if that was the case, what about you? Your chest was empty."

"That's true; perhaps what I want is something it can't give. Perhaps, it's out of the reach of the abyss," David replies.

"So then, what do you want?" Sam asks.

David's face turns a bit depressed, but he still replies, "The cure. Our mom is sick with the statue disease. We started diving to make the money to save her."

Everyone goes quite for a moment until Anthony breaks it. "Sorry for that; I don't think Sam meant to bring up something like that. Regardless, why can't the abyss give you the cure?" Anthony says.

Looking up for a moment, David's face changes to surprise. "Again, this is nothing but an idea, but what if it was on purpose? What if that thing knew what I really, really wanted but chose not to give it to me?

Like it's playing with me; it knows if I get what I want, I won't go into the abyss anymore."

Surprised by his idea, Anthony asks again, "Why would it want you to be here? What would that accomplish?"

"Whatever it wants doesn't matter to me now; it can't stop me from saving my mom," David replies.

Nodding, Sam laughs a little. "Well, looks like you're turning into a little man, huh."

Anthony joins in as well, patting David's back. "You're starting to grow up; if you're not going to let this monster stop you, we won't either."

David blushes a little. "C'mon, you two, it's not that much. Either way, it seems we are only at the mercy of whatever that thing wants. So if we want answers, I guess we have to keep diving."

Finding their resolve, Sam and Anthony both agree they will not let this thing put them down.

CHAPTER 12

THE UNDEAD

Two days have passed from the group's experience with the forest. Today, the pitter-patter of rainfall hitting plastic tents and puddles of water ring out around the camp. The air is full of moisture as the water gathers more and more on the ground, filling in the slightest of holes and divots. People taking shelter from the midday storm, huddle together under the tents. Sheltered, they eat lunch, have a smoke break, or talk amongst themselves. Joseph and Mike are taking time to eat, while the others fix any problems with their gear. David, despite the rain, still trains, currently on a jog. Rounding the corner of the cafeteria again, David notices Joseph reading a paper after finishing his food. Starting to tire out, David makes his way under the cafeteria tent to Joseph.

Wiping the water from his face and catching his breath, David asks Joseph, "What are you reading there?"

"It's a housing pamphlet," Joseph replies.

"A house pamphlet? What, are you moving out already?" David asks.

Nodding, Joseph continues, "I'm thinking about it; with the money we're making, I could do it."

"What about Mom?" David asks, slightly annoyed.

"You're still there, you're taking care of her," Joseph says, in an attempt to brush off David's comment.

"I meant, the money, Joseph; we still need the money to help her," David quickly responds.

Joseph looks up from the paper to David. "We're making enough money; it'll be fine."

With slight anger, David raises his voice a little, "Are we?"

Annoyed by his comment, Joseph responds, "Yes, we are, and everything will be fine."

For a moment, they glare at each other; the air is heavy and wet, and now tense as well.

Walking over to the table, Henry approaches, "Anyone want chicken?"

As the two look over to him, David sighs and tells them he's going to continue running. As he leaves, Joseph looks back down and continues reading. Henry, still standing there, looks over to Mike who's just sitting at the table.

"What did I miss?" Henry asks.

The next day, the group has all gathered together for another dive. Just like every other day, they brave the unyielding darkness, but with more caution than before. Together, they all enter the gate and walk down the same hallway. Once again, the doors are before them; this time all nine are open.

"Strange, I didn't think that many people entered today in the morning. It's only seven, after all," Henry comments.

"At this point, it seems everything is strange, Henry," Anthony says.

Sam leans in between Anthony and Henry, "Wouldn't that make everything normal, Ant?"

Anthony looks over at Sam and quietly ignores her. "Let's just go with this middle one."

As they enter the door, they find the room is filled with rows of tables standing side by side. These tables vary in construction, from ornate complexity to simple wooden boards held together. Under each table, there are open chests; looking around, the group know they have to catch up to whoever entered first. Rushing around, they try to find the way down as fast as possible. All the way to the left wall, Ben finds the door; he calls out and gathers the group. Standing at the top of the stairs, they ready themselves. Going down, they find the next open door; Henry is the first to run through it into a new room. As he runs in, he slams into a square pillar, falling to his back on the floor. Sitting up, Henry rubs his face and looks around. The others following walk in after Henry. Looking around, they find more square pillars coming up from the ground and a little above their heads. Anthony, touching one, discovers they're as wide as Anthony's hand from pinky finger to thumb. The tops of them appear jagged and broken. Some of them stand perfectly straight up. Some lean off into a random direction, others lean on each other, making strange formations. As they investigate, faintly in the distance, David hears a man yell. It's the yell of someone in danger and agonizing pain. Instinctively, David rushes to the source to help. Noticing him run off, the group follow David, calling out to him. As David comes to a halt, another set of stairs are before him. Catching up to him, Anthony asks what made him run off suddenly.

"Someone is in trouble; I heard them yell from over here," David replies.

"Let me take the lead," Joseph says as he pulls out his sword.

Joseph leads the group down. Entering, they hear the familiar pitter-patter of water hitting dirt.

From the back, Henry comments, "I don't remember it raining when we entered the gate."

Collectively, everyone comes to the same conclusion: something is not right.

As they come to the bottom of the stairs, they find the door is wide open. Sword ready, Joseph jumps through, finding a little set of three steps below him. Looking up the group notice it's nighttime, a black sky full of stars in every corner they look, too many stars to even count. It's dark enough to make it hard to notice small details, but the large moon still gives off enough light to see. Looking around, Joseph notices that the door they came through is connected to a building. Examining the building, they find it is burned down and destroyed. It is the remains of the once cozy wooden log house. Walking down the steps to the dirt, the group look around and see many more of these buildings. They are lined up right next to each other, forming a type of dirt street. Ben, being the tallest, looks through a square opening on the wall, peering into one burned building.

"What do you see, Ben?" Sam asks as she walks next to him.

"Bodies," concerned, Ben quietly replies.

Shocked, Sam asks Ben to pick her up to look through the window. Ben lifts Sam up to look through the opening, and they inspect the room full of burned bodies. The bodies litter the destroyed room. In the middle of the room, a rug is still freshly lit on fire, under a pile of the wooden beams from the collapsed roof. Against the furthest wall, there's a bench; sitting on it are two burned bodies, but it's too hard to make out. However, because of the flicker of the fire, Sam can tell one body is a taller person. In the arms of the taller person appears to be a smaller person. Together in their final moments, they were embracing each other. Sam, having seen enough of this death and destruction, asks Ben to put her down. The two walk back together, regrouping with the others.

Anthony, curious by the depressed look on Sam, asks, "What did you guys find?"

"If I had to guess, these are just homes; of course we can't come up with whatever caused all this. However, whatever did all this, did it fast, fast enough that the people had no time to prepare themselves," Sam replies.

Everyone goes silent for a moment, taking in the horrific situation they are surrounded by.

"What could burn what looks like a whole town in what was probably minutes?" Mike asks.

"I don't think we really want to find the answer to that question," David replies.

Anthony speaks up to get everyone's attention. "Alright, either way, let's make our way around the town. One way or another, we're here, so we might as well find something to take back with us."

As the group walks around, they pass a large amount of homes. From the building they entered the town, this placed seemed smaller than what they are finding now. However, as they investigate the town, it begins to get larger and larger. It's building after building from one-story homes to two-story buildings. One building in particular stands out; it's the only three-story building. It's large enough to stand above all the other buildings surrounding it. Getting closer, they find this building sits on the edge of a circular opening. As the group walk through the opening, David pauses, gazing up at the building.

"Why does this look like the library?" David murmurs out.

"What?" Anthony asks.

"This building, it looks almost exactly like the library back home. But that would be impossible; we're in the abyss. Right?" David says.

"Personally, I wouldn't know; never been to the library," Henry says.

"Perhaps it's just a coincidence. If let's say this was built by humans, then it wouldn't be that surprising that we would build the same type of building," Sam says.

"Maybe, but if so, that's a huge coincidence," David replies.

Scanning the rest of the circular opening, the group notice, around the sides, there are small wooden stands just as burned as the homes. The group conclude, this place formed a type of market for the inhabitants of the town. The large building's purpose though is unknown to the group. Turning down one of the dirt roads, the group continue walking between the homes; fire still crackle inside, on, and around them. They provide a dim dancing light as the group moves. Passing by one home, they hear a shuffling noise from under the front of the house. Concerned someone may still be alive, they go to investigate. Ben and Anthony pry away a board resting on the dirt and shoved against the home. Just behind it, they discover a young girl cowering alone in the dark. The young child notices the new opening in her hiding hole, then lets out a small yell. The two, surprised, try to calm her but to no avail. With haste, the girl runs between the two, back down the road and round a corner. David and Joseph attempt to follow her to ensure she's not harmed. However, as they come around the same corner, they find nothing. No trace left behind; the girl got away. The pair continue their search along the road. They look under the homes, even peer into some of them. Disheartened, they end their search; if she was an inhabitant here, she will know many hiding spots. On their return trip, David and Joseph intersect with a woman walking out from between two homes. Shocked to see another person, they start to get closer to her, in hopes of finding out what is happening.

As the two get closer, they can see clearly more of the woman; she is dressed in black robes. On the cuffs of the sleeves, they turn a brilliant white. This stark contrast continues—a bright white band of cloth around her neck on the dress. This band merges with the white around the opening of her hood. All the way down to just above her ankles, the end of the robe turns white as well. As she turns to face the two, they notice she appears strangely clean. For David and Joseph, who only just arrived, within minutes of being here had become dirty. Anyone walking in this large amount of soot, ash, and dust should become dirty. Now they stand face to face, just few steps away. They can see her face and figure more clearly. Her hair is bright blonde; dotted on her face is just one freckle below her left eye. Her face appears quite narrow, tapering to a soft point at her chin. David and Joseph do not know what they should do, so they introduce themselves.

The woman quietly stares at them, looking them up and down. As they talk, she smiles softly, tilting her head to the side. Once they finish their introduction, she speaks; the tone of her voice is soft and sweet; however, the pair can't make out any words she is speaking. Not that they cannot hear but they cannot understand. She does not speak the same as they do; her language is different. Though the two cannot understand her, she strikes the two as a kind and caring person. After a moment, she stops talking, then clasps her hands together, and brings them to her chin. Next, she tilts her head down a little, bowing toward them, then turns around to walk away. Confused, David and Joseph look at each other for just a moment.

"Guess that was some kind of goodbye?" Joseph says.

David shrugs. "Anyway, it looks like we got all turned around; let's get back and find everyone."

Joseph agrees, and they try to make their way back the way they came.

Just after David and Joseph had run off, the others tried to catch up to them. However, they had gone in the wrong direction and lost the two brothers. Now, Anthony and Mike are leading the others around, searching for the two. As they come around another corner, they notice a woman facing a home. Anthony calmly approaches her and begins asking her if she is hurt. Noticing the man, the woman turns and faces the whole group beside her. This woman is dressed in black robes. Her head is adorned with a tall hat that goes to a sharp point; at the base, the brim of the hat is extremely wide. Getting a better look at her, Anthony notices her robes have white markings up and down the sleeves. Most noticeable is how scandalously she is wearing the robes. From her neck to the midpoint of her stomach, she is exposed, with the robes just barely covering any private areas. The robe splits on both sides of either leg on the outside of her thighs. Despite this, she looks at Anthony with no regard to her choice of dress. As she looks at Anthony and the group, her face sours a little, a face full of disgust. Without speaking a word, she brushes some of her blonde hair covering the left half of her face. The woman waves off the group to get away, as if it's something she cannot be bothered with. After ignoring the group, she walks into the house and begins looking around. She looks around the first room before walking off into a side room. Getting the feeling they are not welcome, Anthony turns back to the group. He informs them that the woman could not be bothered with them and that they should continue searching for David and Joseph.

Just a few houses over, David and Joseph continue to try and make their way back. However, the burned down homes provide little to no sense of direction. To the two of them, all the homes look the same. Soon they find themselves back at the circular courtyard. From here, they have a vague idea of where they went. In their attempt to retrace their steps, they are once again lost. In a fit of anger, Joseph kicks one of the pillars leaning against one of the homes just next to them. The vibrations cause the rest of the lone standing pillars to shake loose and begin falling. What was left of the home has now collapsed in on itself, revealing the road that is just next to them, as well as Henry, who's standing on the road. Looking over, Henry waves to David and Joseph.

"Guys, they found me," Henry shouts down the street.

Walking over, the rest of the group are relieved to finally have found David and Joseph. The pair then climb over the debris to the group.

"Where did you guys go?" Anthony asks.

"Well, after chasing the little girl, we eventually lost her around a corner. After searching around, we decided it was probably best to just give up the search," David replies.

"Yeah, it was weird too; just after we decided to head back, we met a woman just wandering around; we couldn't understand each other but she seemed like a nice person at least," Joseph says.

"So you guys met a strange woman too? Just after you two left, while we were looking for you, we also made contact with a woman. Black robes, white highlights on it, exposing too much skin and a big hat," Anthony say.

"Well, almost; she didn't have a hat, she had a hood, and she didn't really expose any skin at all," David replies.

"So they were similarly dressed but not the same; I guess maybe the two women are working together for something," Anthony says.

"You think they caused all this?" Joseph asks.

"I somehow doubt that; despite how annoyed the woman looked, I don't get the feeling she did all this. She looked like, just being here was unpleasant," Anthony replies.

"She was pretty pleasant for me," Henry says.

Ben swiftly smacks the back of Henry's head.

"Thanks, Ben," Sam says.

Henry, rubbing his head, asks, "Anyway, what did the lady say to you because she wasn't in a speaking mood for us?"

David and Joseph shrug.

"We don't know; we couldn't understand her. She spoke in some weird language," David says.

"What do you mean some weird language?" Anthony asks.

"That's just it; she spoke in some language; we don't know what she was saying. Once she finished, she put her hands together, bowed slightly, then left," David replies.

"Well, besides all that, I say we just leave; it feels wrong trying to find any value in this destruction, if there is any value here anymore," Sam says.

Overall, everyone agrees; however Henry, Mike, and Joseph still want to look around. Anthony tries to come to a conclusion that can satisfy both of them.

"Alright, fine; we'll go back to the door and wait for you three there." Anthony pulls out his clock. "It's gotten to 1:34, so take your time, but the less we linger the better," Anthony say.

Splitting up after a short time of walking around, Anthony, David, Sam, and Ben find their door back to the abyss. Ben and Sam both decide that they just want to get back home, so they decide to leave the group. This leaves both David and Anthony waiting at the door as the other three now go around looking for anything of value. Then, Anthony sits on the steps.

"So, do you have any more thoughts on the mysterious woman you met?" Anthony asks.

David takes a moment to think of what he might have left out before.

Taking a seat on the step next to Anthony, he says, "In all of this, she did not seem scared or anything like that or worried about what's going on. She looked kind of sad for what happened to the people. But overall, it just felt like she was searching for something or maybe someone."

"It seems we have something in common. The woman we met seemed the same way, even though it felt like she was annoyed to see us. It felt like she was looking for something or, as you said, someone. But I don't really believe anyone else is really still alive in all of this. Staying on this idea though of two women, I would hazard to guess that with their similar style of dress, along with seeming to have the same goal they might be working together. Who knows, there might even be more of them," Anthony says.

"Well, there was that little girl we saw and tried to find; if she survived, maybe someone else could. Maybe they were looking for that girl," David says.

Nodding, Anthony says, "It's not like we're probably ever going to find out, but it is fun to think about it."

Walking down the dirt road, Henry, Mike, and Joseph talk as they look through building after building.

"So, what do you guys think is still around here? Some kind of rings or necklaces or maybe just some scrap metal?" Mike says.

"Well, at this point, it really just feels like it's only going to end up being just scrap, but I guess that's better than nothing," Joseph replies.

"Oh, my young fools, you have much to learn; just follow me and we will arrive to find some valuables soon," Henry says, interrupting the two.

"What are you talking about, ye old wise man?" Mike asks sarcastically to Henry.

"What I'm talking about is the huge building we all just forgot existed. Just think about it; compared to all of these other buildings, that one stands out against them all. So why does it stand out? Glad you asked. It stands out because it holds great treasure," Henry replies.

"So, we're going somewhere you think some treasure is located? Great," Joseph says, sighing.

"Well, that's the first thing about treasure, isn't it? No one actually knows if it's there or not; it wouldn't be treasure otherwise. Either way, I happen to have good intuition and my intuition is telling me that there is treasure there," Henry says.

Just as Henry finishes, they arrive back to the circular courtyard once again and make their way to the double door entrance of the building. With all the destruction, the hinges of the doors were burned; it took all three of them to move just one door wide enough for them to get in. Walking in, they come to a long open room; decorating the wall are tall windows, now covered in ash and dust. The windows are caked with layers of soot; only thin strands of moonlight can escape into the room. The only other light is the lamps the three have, illuminating enough to walk around.

"Well, now I just feel like I'm back home with all the darkness and sense of foreboding," Mike comments, looking around at the windows.

As they walk, they notice the long benches stretching from the middle of the room to the side walls. They leave a space in the middle to walk down; however, at the end of this long room, there's a chair on an elevated landing. Almost like squares layered on top of each other, they are shrinking in size as they go up, making four steps all around to walk up. Walking up to the chair, not much of anything is special. It's simply a chair; why it's here, the three cannot come to a conclusion. So they choose to ignore it for now and begin looking for a way up, for once.

Adjacent to the chair on both sides are stairs that lead upwards. Henry chooses the left side stairs; not wanting to be left behind, the other two follow. Getting to the second floor, they come to a long hallway with doors on both sides. Just to the left are the other set of stairs that they could have chosen. Deciding to walk down the hallway, Henry decides to open the first door on the right. They come to a room with nothing more than a dresser and bed. Lying next to the bed is a burned body curled up, holding itself. Henry closes the door now.

"I guess, no one's home; let's keep moving," he says, turning around to the other two.

Ignoring the rest of the doors, they all walk to the end of the hallway to the last set of stairs going up. Ascending them, they come to just one lone door, a few steps away from the stairs. Lying on either side of the door are burned bodies. They are encased in what looks like to be some kind of metal armor. Next to them, spears are clasped tightly in their charred hands. However, it seems neither the armor nor weapons were of help, with what happened. Once again, to open the door, it took the full force of all three of them to push. Finally forcing the metal door open, they find nothing but a small room with no windows. In the middle of the room is a small pedestal. Resting on top of the pedestal is a strange orb; this orb appears metallic in texture. However, it strangely moves and flows in all directions like a liquid. Two gold bands, one going vertical, the other going horizontal around the orb, form a cross at the top and again at the bottom. These bands act like a brace for the orb and keep it still. All three of them walk up to the orb and surround it, silently observing it. Mike is the one who decides to go and touch it. Grasping it in the palm of his hand, he holds it up for them to look closer. As they take in its enchanting swirling and flowing, the gold bands burst into bright light. The bands disappear and with them, the metal liquid falls into Mike's hand. Through his fingers and over the edges, the metal liquid falls to the ground and dissolves into nothing. All three of them look at the ground and watch this happen. Henry looks up at Mike.

"Well, there went our treasure, Mike," Henry says.

Shrugging, Mike responds, "How was I supposed to know the magic orb of magic treasure would dissolve. I know you were thinking of picking it up too."

"Yeah, I was total—" Henry's reply is stopped by a sudden monstrous shriek from outside.

All three of them turn to look at the door. Reaching out from the opening, the thin charred hand reaches to grab the opening of the door. Final bits of flesh fall off it as it easily pushes open the door to its fullest. Standing before them, the body that should have been burned and dead from outside walks again—branding the broken metal plate armor, holding the spear, ready to fight. Shocked, the three pull out their swords, readying themselves.

Anthony and David are still at the steps of the door, talking. Suddenly, David shoots up, standing there looking around.

"What? What did you notice?" Anthony asks.

"Quiet for a moment," David says, pausing for a moment. "Do you hear that it's shuffling from all around us? Something is moving," David finishes.

Quietly, Anthony listens. "No, I don't hear anything," Anthony replies.

David pulls out his sword. "It might be best if you do the same," David says.

In an instant, the town feels as if it has come alive. The rubbles of the homes start shifting in large sections; now the noise is unavoidable. The door across from them on the adjacent home flies open with ease. Standing in the doorway is the corpse of a man, brandishing a rusty damaged sword. His body's burned and black and there are holes in his skin; you can see straight through. As he looks up at David, the clicking and grinding of his bones follow. Face to face with David, his eyes are pure crimson red and sunken into his skull. Half of his face is charred while the other half taken by exposed bone. Glaring at David, his jaw hangs slightly off level as the loud guttural yell leaves its throat. This prompts Anthony to pull out his sword and ready himself against this thing next to David. However, as he gets ready, the doors of the homes next to them swing open. More of these monsters pour out of the homes, some even smash through the walls. David backs up to be shoulder to shoulder with Anthony as the monster across the street from them steps down the stairs. Surrounded now, the two look at each other.

"We hold out until the others get back; they could be in danger as well," Anthony says.

David nods, steeling himself for a fight.

Back inside the room, Joseph stands steadfast as the monster runs at him, flailing the pole from side to side, then up and down, thrusting, retracting, and thrusting again. Joseph watches this and moves out of the way as each swing comes at him. From some blows, Joseph shields himself with his sword. The force of the impact demonstrates the monster's strength but no follow up shows off the monster's lack of skill. However, with his skill, Joseph manages to get close enough to hit the monster with his sword. Slashing across the chest, the sword meets with the monster's metal plate, letting out a loud clang. Joseph simply lets out a hmm before backing off, as the monster attacks once again.

"Hit him in the head," Mike yells.

"I know that now, thanks," Joseph responds.

Just as before, the monster swings wildly in all directions; Joseph dodges the swings, aiming his sword edge for the head. Cleaving the head right off the body, the monster falls to ash and disappears. His metal chest plate clangs on the ground along with his spear right next to him.

"Well, at least it can die. Again, I guess," Joseph says, looking down at the ash.

Joseph, leading the others out the room, ducks just at that split moment another spear comes hurling from the side. Standing there gripping the spear in hand, the second body the group had forgotten about. However, the sharp end of the pole embedded itself in the wall, giving Mike the chance to slice off the head of the second one.

"What, didn't feel like a haircut today?" Henry comments to Joseph crouched down.

"No, Mom always said I look good with longer hair," Joseph replies.

Free from the monsters, they walk down the stairs, back to the hallway. They find all of the doors open with the bodies from each room standing ready for them in the middle of the hallway.

Joseph sighs. "Well, at least they don't have weapons and armor. I'll go first; Mike, you're next, then, Henry, you follow up."

"Wait, what do you mean?" Henry asks, confused.

Without answering, Joseph charges at the first monster, chopping its head off. Coming up behind Joseph, Mike shoves the monster to the wall, then slices the head off. Henry, finally understanding what Joseph meant, runs past the two and stabs one monster in the chest. As he drives the sword deep through the monster, he thinks he has killed it. However, in Henry's moment of victory, the monster glares down at Henry. It raises its arm high up and brings it down, smashing Henry in the face, knocking him to the ground. Joseph, sweeping in, chops the head off, then looks over to Henry.

"It seems you have to go for the head to do anything to these things," Joseph says, extending his hand to Henry.

Henry grabs his hand and stands back up, rubbing his face and bleeding nose.

"Well, they sure ain't messing around," Henry mutters as he grabs his sword.

Mike comes through again, dealing with the next monster. Mike calls to the other two. "C'mon, let's get out of here fast, then have a friendly chat."

Back to back, Anthony and David stand in the middle of the road. More and more of theses monsters appear to come out of the woodwork, like flood. As they stand there turning round and round, they do their best to face every direction.

"So you think they're maybe friendly and just misunderstood based on their appearance?" Anthony asks.

On David's side, one monster in the very back of the crowd picks up a thin long pole of wood. The monster brings it up next to his face, aiming it upwards, then throws it at the two.

"Move to the left!" David yells to Anthony.

The pair jump in opposite directions; in between the two, the pole lands, jabbing the ground with force. David looks at the pole embedded in the ground.

"I said left," David says.

"This was my left," Anthony says.

Standing back up, they once again turn back to back; they each swing their swords at the monsters; however, they miss, falling short of any monster's faces.

"I thought you know how to use that," Anthony says.

Annoyed, David answers, "I never really trained to use it; what about you? You're older."

"Hey, I never had any opportunity to, you know, do all this crazy stuff," Anthony replies.

David and Anthony slowly shift, turning in an attempt to keep every monster at bay but to avail. There are too many to see all of them at once;

they fill the road like the ocean. Soon, the monsters begin moving one foot after another and step ever closer. David makes a wild swing for one's head, but it blocks it with its own sword. In this brief moment, it feels as if the monster is looking down at him, laughing at his weak feeble attempt at a sword swing. Angry, David retracts his sword just enough to move it away from the block and thrusts forward, piercing straight through the monster's head; as he pulls out the sword, the monster falls to ash. All at once, the monsters stop, look over at David, and begin charging at the two. Surprised, Anthony and David begin fighting for their lives. Anthony blocks most of the attacks coming at him, then retaliates one monster at a time. David tries to dodge any attack; most of the attacks are not fatal. Some land a scratch here and there but nothing David cannot keep up with. Swinging the sword, David occasionally overswings and misses some swings entirely. A few attacks David tries to block; all they accomplish are a few dents in the sword's edge. David can feel it; if he were to be any weaker, the sword would have come out of his hands by now. These monsters throw full power into every attack. Their aggression and speed makes them dangerous foes. However, their lack of accuracy allows the two to keep up. Anthony and David hold on and try to thin this herd of monsters together.

Charging out the large doors of the building, Joseph, Mike, and Henry have traded one bad situation for another. The once-dead lifeless town center has come alive. Every direction they look, monsters stand armed and ready. The three are already tired just from getting out of the building. Now they have a whole town between them and the exit. Looking around, Joseph searches for the road they came down. Wiping the sweat from his brow, Joseph takes out his compass.

Looking down at the needle, Joseph shouts, "This way, don't worry about any of these things that don't stand in our way."

Charging forward, he runs headfirst down the road, followed by Mike and Henry, who are struggling to keep up. As the group moves, any monster directly in front get a taste of a blade. They dodge and move out of the way of any attacks coming from the sides. Finally they can see a group of monsters with their backs to them. Soon, as they carve their way through them, the sound of metal clashing can be heard. As they make their way to the center, they find Anthony and David fighting. Glad they have made their way out of this madness, they call out to them. Noticing them between sword strikes, David warns them to be careful of their surroundings. As they carve closer and closer, Mike trips on the pole that was thrown earlier. Joseph stops, turning around to help Mike up. Looking up from his knees, Mike just in time notices it in the air behind Joseph. Another pole is heading for them to Mike's exact spot next to the other pole. In a quick split-second decision, instead of holding onto Joseph's hand, he grabs it. Mike shoves Joseph to the side, just in time for Joseph to dodge the pole and for it to impale Mike through the chest. Lying on the floor, Joseph looks up and his face fills with horror.

"No!" he yells out.

Henry grabs Joseph by the shoulder and helps him up, "C'mon, we have to leave."

"We can't leave Mike; we have to help him," Joseph shouts, hesitating to go with Henry.

Henry looks over at Mike who's still on his knees getting swarmed by the monsters as they raise their weapons ready. Henry looks away and down to Joseph.

"We can't help him; we need to leave," Henry says.

He then pulls Joseph away from the one-sided massacre of his friend. They enter the circle created by Anthony and David.

"Where's Mike?" David asks.

Henry only shakes his head and looks down to Joseph. Josephs face stricken with grief as both tears and sweat pour down his face.

David looks over to Anthony. "You help them to the door; I can hold on for a bit."

Hearing the determination in his voice, Anthony breaks off, making a path to the door. Henry, carrying Joseph, still tries to swing his sword with his free hand to aid Anthony. David, backing up with every attack, ensures no other monster gets around them. Finally reaching the door, Anthony grabs Joseph and Henry, flinging them into the door.

Standing by the side of the door, Anthony calls out to David, "Hurry up; they're in."

Turning to a full sprint, David gives his back to the monsters. This opening allows for one last attack to make it through, a cut across the back of David's right shoulder. As David falls through the door, Anthony leaps in after him. Strangely, the darkness of the abyss feels welcoming.

The group, together again, are lying at the base of the stairs, catching their breath and resting. David tries to hold onto his wound but cannot quite reach over that far. Anthony comes over to investigate it; holding his lamp up, he looks at the wound.

"It's not a deep cut; your clothes added some protection but you should be fine; let's get out of here, when we all catch our breath," Anthony says to David.

Groaning in pain, David stands up along with the others. Joseph is wiping the tears away and cleaning his nose. Beaten and tired, the group move through the abyss the same way they came in, eventually reaching the end and coming out from another dive mostly intact.

Leaving the gate, the group find Sam and Ben who were waiting for them to return. Walking over to them, Sam apologizes for leaving them, clarifying they just did not feel safe.

"You should be," Joseph replies coldly as he walks past.

Surprised, the two of them look back at Joseph because of his reaction. However, in the moment, they let it go, turning back to the group noticing Mike is gone. Ben goes and helps Anthony tend to David's wound, while Sam pressures Henry for answers of what happened down there.

Henry explains everything that they experienced from the building down to when Mike was killed. Shocked, Sam can only just apologize even more.

"It's not your fault, Sam; you didn't kill him. Besides, this is all the nature of the abyss anyway. Every dive we take, we put our lives on the line, we should all know that from the start. This is just a reminder that we could die at any time," Anthony says, interrupting Sam's apologies.

"The nature of the abyss? Ant, nothing about this is natural! I came here to look around in the dark for stuff and get rich. Sure I know death lurked everywhere but th-this isn't the abyss anymore," Henry says.

Sam looks over at Anthony. "For once, I agree with Henry; nothing like this has ever happened to anyone. While you guys were down there, we asked people what they experienced. Everyone says the same thing: nothing out of the ordinary; this is just us and we don't know why."

Anthony tries to speak up again but is surprisingly interrupted by Ben. "Please stop fighting here and now; David is wounded," Ben says.

The three look over to David sitting on the floor still bleeding while Ben holds some rags over it to stop.

Collecting himself, Anthony speaks again after a few breaths, "Ben's right; let's help David first. We can argue about what's going on later; let's get him to the medical tent."

Ben and Anthony hoist David up together and walk him to a tent to get treated. Now more than ever, the group can feel it in the back of their minds. Whatever is happening is taking its toll on them and has collected its first prize.

CHAPTER 13

VISIT

Four days have gone by from Mike's death; to the group, these four days felt like the longest days they have ever experienced. For David, he decided it was best to stay at home, read some books, talk to his mother, and rest his wound. David, sitting on his couch in the large room in his home, is reading a new book he picked up from the library. His mother sits just in front of him, looking out the window as she always does. To break the deafening silence, David's mother turns to David.

"So, what are you reading this time, anything interesting?" she asks.

David, more than willing to oblige, begins telling her of the book's story: the fictional adventures of a group of explorers in a wild unknown forest, full of forgotten tombs. The usual stuff that David enjoys reading, fiction and fantasy, with the occasional book of knowledge, the only escape from this dreadful life he may ever get. His mother grins happily as her son retells the events of the story and all the adventures this band of adventurers go on. As David finishes his retelling of the events that he has read up to, his mother changes the topic.

"That sound like a very nice book. Have you made any progress with the girl there?" David's mother asks.

"What?" David asks.

"You know, have you talked to her more, maybe even invited her out to spend time together or something?" his mother replies.

"I don't really have the time to be doing any of that, Mom," David says, hiding his face in his book.

"Well, what are you doing right now?" his mother asks.

"Reading," David replies.

"So, you could have been reading with that girl right now," his mother says.

"She's working, so we couldn't have and I wouldn't want to read at the library; that would be distracting," David says.

"Distracting for who?" his mother asks.

"Her, obviously," David replies as he flips a page in his book.

"Hmm, okay; well then, putting that aside, have you been to Joseph's new home yet?" his mother asks.

"No, not yet," David replies.

"You should, maybe he'll have a spare room you could move into," David's mother says.

"And what about you? You'll be here all alone," David retorts.

David's mother huffs. "Such is the way of being a parent; you raise your children into adults, and they leave to go on with their lives and so on," his mother says.

"And what about your sickness? If I'm spending money on rent, I won't have enough money to save you," David replies.

"So I die," David's mother says, brushing his concerns.

Angry, David raises his voice a little, "And I don't want you to die; I don't want anyone to die."

David's mother looks at him sharply, quieting him down for a moment.

"Do you think I'm immortal? Do you think any one of us is immortal? As much as I enjoy these stories along with you, David, you have to live in the real world. You have to go out and enjoy your life that you have. Go and do all the things you can and want to do. Don't be stuck in the past, trying to kill yourself working in these factories for me. Life goes by so much faster than you think it will. We all die, I will die, you will die, everyone dies; that is something we cannot stop. At the very least, I could die happy, knowing that you are living a fulfilling life and not one trying to hold onto the past. Go and live a little, move out, have fun, talk more with that girl you like at the library. Live your life; that's all I want," David's mother says.

David closes his book and stands up. "I promise I'll live my life, when I get the money to cure you and I will cure you," he says.

David's mother begins shaking her head. "Of course, of course, well, I'm going to get some sleep now."

David begins to leave the room. "Then while you sleep, I'm going out for a little bit." David says as he waves her goodbye.

Walking down the narrow alleyways, for David, recently they feel as if they have begun to shrink. However, for now, David makes his way to Housing District 54. This district in itself is not impressive but for the two brothers who lived in 57, it's an improvement. Trying to gather himself, David puts on his best to be happy for Joseph moving out. Even though he would disagree with the choice, he knows it's best to be happy for him in the end. Regardless of all of David's feelings about this, he still makes his way to Joseph's home.

Passing various different housing districts David never thought he would enter, despite the fact that he lived so close the entire time. Entering District 57 now, David pulls out a small crumpled up piece of paper he had written Joseph's address on. Looking around, David realizes he does not know how to get there. Despite the fact that the streets look and function identically, the names and buildings are unknown to David. Everything here is foreign to him, so he takes a breath in, then finds someone to ask. Walking over to an older gentleman who's smoking a cigarette in front of a building, David asks him for directions. Politely, the man points him in the direction David needs to go. As he follows the man's directions, David believes he is heading the correct way. After a few corners, he realizes he is once again lost. Sighing, David once again asks another stranger for directions, this time, an elderly woman sitting down knitting on some steps to a home. Kindly, she stops for a moment, looks up at David, and begins telling him extremely detailed directions. Even though the woman means well for David, she is going into much greater detail than he has the need to know. The woman talks about which light posts to look for, she describes the surrounding buildings down to the cracks in the foundations. David is sure the woman even described the cracks in the ground to watch out for, so he doesn't trip. Overwhelmed with knowledge, David politely attempts to ask her to make the directions more simple and understandable for him. She kindly accepts and gives David simple left, right, or straight directions. Finally understanding where to go, David thanks the kind old woman and leaves to be on his way to Joseph's house.

After what felt like hours to David, he has made his way to the front steps of Joseph's small home. From the outside, not much has changed from where he used to live. The alleyways are small no wider than two person's shoulder width apart. Looking up, David finds three other homes rest on top of Joseph's ground-floor home. Looking down now, he finds three simple small steps lead up to a sunken door into the wall. Knocking on the door, David waits for a moment; faintly on the other side, he can hear rustling. Soon, the noises stop, then footsteps start; they get louder and louder. Soon, Joseph opens the door, greeting David.

"Hey, Dave, you stopped by," Joseph says, leading his arm inward to the house. "C'mon in, no need to stand in the doorway."

Taking a few steps into Joseph's home, David feels as if he stepped into a smaller version of his own home. One large room to his immediate left, just down the hallway, two doors, one on either side. The only difference David can pick out is, in the large room, the window is moved to a different wall. The window is just next to the door in the large room; other than this minute change, nothing stands out. However, Joseph still decides to give David the tour of the home, walking into the large room first. Along the wall adjacent to the room's entry, is an old couch that came with the home. To its left in the corner of the room is David's diving gear that Mike had previously been holding onto. Now that responsibility to keep this a secret from their mother falls on Joseph. Onto its right side, the room turns into a small kitchen, the same basic appliances that David has in his mother's home. Not much else sits in the room; no table lamps or chairs just yet. Turning around and leaving the room, Joseph beckons David to keep following him. Going down the hallway, the door on the right, as David expected, is the bathroom. Nothing more than a toilet, shower, and sink, and just as expected, the walls are cracked just as much as the rest of the home. Turning around, the other door leads to Joseph's room; on one side of the room is his old bed that he took. To the right is a tall person sized dresser; opening it, Joseph shows off his storage for all his diving gear. On the left, his backpack hangs, sitting in the middle, his lamp and other accessories, then hanging on the right, his gold sword. Joseph sits on his bed; raising his hands, he gestures to the whole room.

"So, what do you think, Dave? Pretty cool, right?" Joseph says.

Taking a moment, David looks around. "Well, it is," David says as he looks up at the cracks in the ceiling. "Nice," David finishes as he looks back to Joseph. "Anyway, Joseph, thank you for showing me around, but I just wanted to say something."

Putting a hand up to stop David, Joseph interrupts him. "I know, I know, and it's okay. I'm doing fine after Mike died; buying this house kept reminding me that this is life and life moves on; that's all we can do," Joseph says.

Rubbing the back of his neck, David replies, "Well, that's all good and all, but I wanted to talk about the money, you know the money for Mom. To save her."

Joseph looks at David, smiling for a moment. "Of course, the money to save Mom. I can't really give any at the moment, you know with the house and all, but when we start diving again, I promise I will pitch in."

David nods his head a little. "Right, yeah, but anyway, if you have the time, you can just put it in my safe box instead of having to come to give it to me. It's up on the hill below the tree. I, we don't need much more money for Mom, and when that's all done, you can keep diving, but I want to go back to work. Normal work that is," David says.

Standing up, Joseph clasps David's shoulders. "Yeah, Dave, I know we don't have long, so I guarantee that in the next few dives, we'll have the money needed to save Mom. Me and you can do this together," Joseph says.

"Well, any help is helpful so; anyway, I have to return this book, so I'll see you next week, Joseph," David says as he looks around.

Bringing his hands down, Joseph nods. "I'll see you next week, Dave, when you're all healed up," Joseph says.

As David leaves the room, Joseph trails behind, waving goodbye as David leaves the front door. After his brief visit, David decides its best to just head home for now and rest.

CHAPTER 14

THE TOWN

One week has passed from the day Joseph moved out of the house. David has recovered from his wound and has readied himself for just a few more dives. Taking a moment to look back and reflect over this week, David begins to wonder, Was all this really the best solution? Things change, he knows this, but they don't feel like they are changing for the better. The only thing that helps David keep going is the reality of his goal is so close to his grasp. With every minor dive, he feels like he has gone one step forward; however, every time a major incident in the abyss happens, he feels like he has moved three steps back. Sitting under his tree, David just keeps repeating to himself, "Don't stop, don't stop." With every repetition, the world feels like its crumbling ever so slightly more.

Picking himself up, David stands to ready himself for the day; just as he had done before he makes his way to the docks, onto the boat, then up the beach to the gate. Tired still, David takes one moment to stand in front of the gate and looks up. When this all started, David felt fear looking up at this behemoth; now he can't really feel anything for it. It simply just exists to David now; this object is nothing more than part of the background.

Kicking him out of his trance, Anthony pats David on the shoulder, "So you ready to rejoin us today?"

Looking over at him, David nods his head, then follows Anthony to join up with the group. Standing to the side of the gate, Joseph, Sam, Ben, and Henry are waiting for the two to join them. Approaching the group, David greets them, relieved to see them after his week-long hiatus. Readying themselves, the group once again follow their way into the eerie darkness. Anthony, as always, leads the group. Their exploration so far has been quiet, even Henry does not have much to say. As they come to the first set of doors, seven await them. Six of the seven are open. Looking them over, the group thinks; finally, Henry speaks up a little.

"You guys ever feel like something is messing with us?" Henry groans.

"All the time," David replies, sighing at the end.

Anthony interrupts them. "Well, either way, we only have one choice, so let's get on with it."

"Technically, we have eight choices," Henry quips.

"Henry, we only have seven doors; what's the eighth option?" Sam asks

"We could leave," Henry replies.

After his statement, the group quietly looks over at Henry. Anthony proceeds to open the door and walks in. Following his lead, the others do the same. Henry, left alone, can only shrug to himself, then begins following the group. Entering the door, they expected to find a room or stairs. The group never expected to find a hallway. As they walk down it, they are left unfazed by this strange occurrence. After the many unusual things going on, the group doesn't think much can surprise them now. The hallway comes to an end with nothing more than a stone wall. No way to proceed forward, it looks like to the group. Anthony turns around to face the group to tell them, there is no way to continue. However, as he faces them, no words escape his mouth. The group stares at Anthony, wondering what he was going to say. Without any words, Anthony motions to the group with his hands to turn around. Curious, they do so; what greeted them when they turned was a completely empty room. Looking around in bewilderment, Henry asks where the hallway went. Not knowing how they got here, the group spreads out and searches for a way out. They attempt to find anything that resembles a door, stairs, or even the hallway again. Moments of separation, regrouping, separating, and regrouping over and over. Joseph, in a small fit of rage, stomps one foot on the ground. He then proceeds to yell at the darkness to stop toying with them. When Joseph's ranting is over, David asks if he would like to continue searching. Joseph huffs, then agrees to keep looking.

Eventually after two hours of walking in circles, the group comes to a halt, taking a moment to think and pull together any ideas one may have. No one in the group can come up with anything; they all come to the same conclusion. How could they think of a way out; they're dealing with something beyond them. Something no one could hope to understand. Something that defies all reality and thought. Soon, a glimmer of despair starts to form and take hold. Perhaps, they thought, there is no way out. Perhaps their lives end here and now. In an attempt to stop such despairing thoughts, Henry takes a moment away from the group. As he fades into the darkness, the dimness of his lamp light fades into nothing. David, listening, can no longer hear Henry's footsteps. Standing up, David looks in the direction Henry went, gets the group's attention, and tells them, he no longer thinks Henry is here. Shocked, the rest stand up, and Anthony asks for him to tell them what he means.

"I said, I don't think Henry is here anymore, in this room," David clarifies.

"Well, where do you think he went and how?" Anthony asks.

"I'm not sure but I think it seems if we spread out alone, we might find out," David tells the whole group.

Looking around in thought, Anthony agrees, "Okay, so we separate and find our way from there."

"Hold on, hold on; you want us to go alone into whatever this all is?" Sam interrupts Anthony.

"You got a way out of here?" Anthony continues.

Finally, no one has any more objections or questions. They all agree to separate, figure out where they are, and make it back home. For David, the moment they all lose sight of one another, in one blink, everything changes. This time, it's dusk out and the sun is just falling on the horizon. David stands right where a lush forest and rolling plains meet. Out in the middle of the grassy plains is a town surrounded by wooden walls. The road leading to the front gate is lined with people, all of them waiting to get inside the town. David is surprised that the town is alive this time. The technology appears slightly more primitive than what David is used to. The town buildings are made of large stones and wood. Along the road, next to the people are some wooden squares. They are held up by what looks like wooden gears to David. In front of them are four-legged creatures, roughly the height of humans. They're tied to the square, for what purpose, David doesn't know. After a minute, the line moves and the creatures move forward to pulling the square. Although curious about why there is such a gap in technology, David decides to not think about it. After all, he has a more important matter, like getting out of here, wherever here is. The forest line is atop a small hill, so David can see farther but not like it would help. Past the town and all around it looks to be just more forest line. For a moment, David did think of going into the town. However, after the last encounter with a person, he thinks the language barrier might exist here too. So David votes against going into the town. He leans up against a tree to rest and think for a moment. Suddenly, rustling is heard behind him turning around David readies himself to confront whatever is making these noises. Sticks snapping, leaves rustling louder and louder. Soon, a patch of bushes separate and falling out between them is a man. However, he looks like a man but not so much. The man is covered head to toe in metal. Even his head is surrounded in a cylinder-shaped metal piece. Attached to his neck and flowing down to his shins is a pure white cloth. As the man stands up, he rests two heads taller than David. His height rivals that of the gate commander who was tall enough already. David takes note of his metal suit adorned with symbols on his shoulders and chest. Parts of the metal seems worn and beaten and scratches align every part. On his hip, David can see the outline of a sword being holstered, as well as a longer sword outline on his back under the cloth. Looking over, he sees two slits sit on the metal where his face should be. His head tilts down to look at David. Then he speaks; however, just like the woman from before, he can't understand him. David, listening, thinks that even though he can't understand, this man's speech is different. To David, it just sounds different from the woman, like a completely new language. This brings up more questions, but for now, David has the thought that the two do not exist in the same place. While thinking about this, David notices the man rubbing the metal where his chin should be. To David , it looks like the metal man is also lost in thought. The man looks over to the forest he left and draws his sword from his hip. He gestures to David to stand back with him as he backs away from the forest. Curious, David does the same; after a minute, loud thumps can be heard from the forest.

Trees start to fall as the thumping gets louder and louder. The thumping begins to sound more akin to heavy footsteps, David assumes this is what the man ran away from. Slowly, the man still moves back one step at a time. He looks back and forth from the forest to David. Then quickly sheaths his sword and gestures to David to follow him. After this exchange of hand signals, the man begins running off into the plains. David looks back at the forest, back to the man, then the forest again. Crashing through the tree line, a giant monster, the size of the trees, comes hurling out. It's size and weight are enough to make depressions into the hard ground. David begins running as fast as his legs can carry him, catching up with the man. Soon, screaming can be heard from the people on the road as they scatter to rush into the town. Some drop their belongings, others rush picking up their children. Inside the town, bells can be heard, men yelling to each other on the wall. David and the man run onto the road and toward the town. The people are almost inside, the monster close on their heels. As they get closer to the gate of the town, a flash of light shoots out from the top of the wall. Looking up, David notices it's some kind of ball of fire headed straight for the monster. It clashes dead center on the monster's face, staggering it for a split moment. Regaining its balance, David watches as it wipes the soot from its large red and black eyes. The pupils look like red drops of blood surrounded by an empty darkness. Most importantly, now they're full of rage as the monster lets out a deep roar. David and the man both panic and try to run even faster. Trailing just behind, the monster swings, hitting the wood squares out of the way. One step after another, the monster crushes all the leftover belongings. As the two reach near the gate, the last of the people have made their way inside. Leaving one door just open enough for them to get in, the other men in metal prepare to close the gate. Together, David and the man jump through the gate. As the others slam it shut, the monster can be heard outside roaring in frustration. The men on the wall begin pelting the monster with sharp wooden sticks flung from another piece of wood with a string. One other cloaked figure on the wall begins creating balls of fire just like the previous one. Lying on the floor, David looks up and notices the figure in the cloak creating the fire from symbols. These symbols are bright fire-red and they bare a stark resemblance to the symbols casting the small flames to light the inside of the monster's cave behind the water fall.

Taking a moment to breathe, David thinks back to that cave. The fire on the wall looked like it was coming from the same symbols. The symbols this person is using, however, appears different, more complex. Additionally, the fire that comes out is much bigger and dangerous now. Sitting up, the metal man stands over David, looking down at him. Walking over to them are more men in metal but not as covered. David can see their faces, and they seem to be talking to the metal man. Without understanding what the people are saying, David can understand they are talking about him. They occasionally point at him and talk to the man wearing metal. However, what they are talking about, David does not know. Do they want to get rid of him, kill him, or blame him for the monster? Regardless, David could not go anywhere if he wanted to. That monster is still out there, being fended off outside the wall.

As he's trying to think of his own plan out of here, David's attention is diverted by the man in metal. The man stands there pointing to David, then he points to his sword. He repeats this back and forth pointing until David believes he wants something. So David unsheathes his sword and stands by the man. The man nods his rounded head, then picks up a stick. Kneeling down to the ground, the man begins using the stick to draw something. Soon David realizes the man has drawn a crude version of the monster. After the poor drawing is done, he points to himself, to David, to their swords, and finally the monster. Nodding, David confirms he understands that the man wants David's help killing the monster. The man nods as well; a common understanding has been made. Now the man points to himself and to the right foot of the monster. He then points to David and the left foot of the monster. It appears to David that the man will attack from the right while David attacks the left. However, the man seems to make special care in pointing to cutting the foot. So he points to it on himself, just behind the foot and above the heel. David understands there seems to be a specific place he should cut, so he nods, agreeing. For David, one way or another, he believes the man knows what he's doing. David decides to just follow the metal man's lead; once they're safe, then David can find his way out of here.

Following the metal man, David is led to the gate. Just beyond it is the thumping and roaring of the monster trying to knock the wall down. However, for the time being, the wall seems to hold, for how long though is uncertain. Just above them, the soldiers throw more and more at the monster. Flaming ball after another, the monster just keeps taking it all within its fit of rage. Now just behind the gate, the man readies his sword as he stands against the gate. Just behind him, David stands, just as ready waiting for the man to charge out. As the seconds tick by, the man freezes, appearing to listen steadily, visualizing what is going on behind the gate. Finally, after one specific moment, he creaks the door open and sprints out; David is quick to follow his lead. As the monster clears its eyes from another fireball, he just notices the two running for his feet. The monster, forced into making a quick split-second decision, attempts to attack the metal man. The monster swings the tree trunk in its hand as a club, for it to come crashing down toward the man. The man jumps and rolls out of the way, just steps away from being flattened into the ground. As the man stands back up, he continues sprinting toward the foot. With both hands occupied, the monster forces its foot high into the air. Now with its foot directly above the man, it begins hurdling down to him. However, the monster's mistake was, forgetting there are two attackers. At the same time when the monster attempts to step on the man, David makes his way to his target. As David gets to the foot, without hesitation, he digs the edge of his sword into the monster's flesh. With all of his might, he tries to force the blade further and further in. This single attack is taking all of David's strength.

What is with this skin? It's too soft for the sword to grab it, David thinks to himself. *I have to do this, or we could be killed; I have to do someth*—he cuts off his own thoughts.

David comes to the conclusion: if the sword will not go in, just add more force to it. Taking one hand off the hilt of the sword, David raises it and balls it into a fist. Quickly aligning his knuckles with the blade, he forces his fist into it. He then punches the sword blade. Although this cuts his fist at the same time, the force needed was found. Yelling out in pain, David's cries are soon met with the monster's cry. The sword had successfully penetrated the thick skin and cut deep into the monster's heel. This attack stopped the monster from stomping on the man, forcing his other foot down to support his weight from falling. But this action had sealed the monster's fate. Where David struggled, the man did with ease. As the man slices at the heel like a hot knife, the monster roars out in pain again, falling to its knees. The advantage held now by the man in metal, David watches the magnificent display of precision. Now the man runs back up the length of the monster. On his way to the head, the man cuts the back of the knee, forcing the monster to fall again. Now the monster is practically lying on its side, trying to push itself up with its arms. However, the man is not giving it a chance to recover. His brutally precise attacks never stop. He slices along the back as he runs, cutting deeper and deeper with each swing. Finally reaching the hand, he cuts along the wrist; the monster loses all strength and falls to its face. The man lunges up, raising his sword high into the sky. With great speed, his sword comes down heavy like a guillotine. Standing up straight, the man leans his head back, basking his face in the sun while he takes a moment to catch his breath. Impressed, David walks over to the man; during his walk down the body, the cheers of the citizens can be heard over the wall. The soldiers on the wall also cry out in joy; they appear to wave down to the man, congratulating him, most likely also thanking him. David cannot understand them still but can understand the happiness and joy they are in right now for saving their lives. He stands before the metal man now; the man's head tilts down and he speaks; David believes he might be thanking him. When he finishes, the man reaches out his hand to David. Understanding what he wants, David grabs his hand, shaking it, a show of respect, acknowledging two warriors saving a whole town. As their hands separate, the man reaches over to his side, pulling out a small pouch filled with something metallic, as it clangs around. The man places the pouch in David's hand, presumably a gift for his help. Thinking it to be rude to decline a gift, David accepts it, thanking the man, even though he may not understand David. Curious, David opens the small bag; it's full to the brim with small gold coins. Surprised, David picks one up to investigate it further. The astonishing amount of detail on such a small object leaves David in awe. Engravings of flowers wrapped in vines over a castle on one side; as he flips it over, he finds an extrusion of a man's face jutting out from the coin. David places the coin back with the others, then looks up, beginning to thank the man even more for such a generous gift. However, as David looks up, nothing stands before, no man, no field, no wooden wall, no monster body. Nothing more than darkness filled with silence; somehow David made his way back to the abyss.

David, walking in the darkness aimlessly, feels as if he's going in circles, not moving forward at all. Slowly, a thick dark viscous liquid flows over the stone floor, falling into each crack and hole. Distinctly remembering where David has seen this before, he hides away the pouch of coins into his pocket, then draws his sword. Turning from one side to the next, David looks to his left, right, and left. He can hear it moving around, sloshing, sliding like water taken over by darkness. Unnerved, David yells into the darkness, asking what it wants, why this thing is here. Slowly, it starts in the distance, evil maniacal laughter, until it gets louder and louder, and the laughter comes from every direction. The deep guttural sound of multiple voices speaking over one another but saying the same thing has come again. Its laughter fills David's ears.

"You. Are. Powerless. You meddle in things you don't understand. None of you will live long. After all, I already have one. Five more to claim. All will be mine soon," the darkness silently laughs to itself.

David's voice trembles, "W-why are y-you doing this? What have I done? What have we done?"

"Your crime? Is simply existing while I do. But our fun will continue. Later," the darkness replies, then subsequently draws back out of view into the black void.

David, concerned that this monster left so quickly, checks his belongings. He pats himself down feeling everything he entered with. The darkness has not taken anything yet. To David, it seems the darkness only showed up to toy with him. While putting everything back,

David's watch falls out, opening as it hits the floor. Picking it up, David takes a look at the time while he has it. Soon his face becomes ghost-white as horror fills him. This must be why the monster left right now: 5:48. Two minutes before the flame comes from the bottom of the abyss. Two minutes before David is left to burn alive. Packing everything, David launches into sprint, not caring where, just having to move. Tring to find anything, a door, stairs, something. He keeps an eye on the clock in his hand: 5:49. One more minute. David needs to find something, anything at this point. Soon, he comes to a screeching halt; there's a large hole in the ground, the first anyone has seen. Across from it, it looks like there is more floor, but the gap is too wide; he doubts he can jump it. Looking left, then right, he finds the hole stretches into the darkness. David has to choose a direction, left or right. He just holds his head down, then runs to the right, hoping he made the correct decision. Nothingness after nothingness, there's no way over the hole. As the clock strikes 5:50, David, left with no other option, puts all his energy into leaping over the hole. Slamming into the other side on his chest, he pushes down on the floor, hoisting himself up. Rolling over, he lays there, panting, breathing, slightly excited that he managed to do that. However, his excitement is squashed when he hears the faint laughter again coming from the hole he jumped. Kneeling down over the hole, David sees a light in the distance. Distracted by the light, a black tendril flings itself from the other side of the hole, grabbing David. Its intention felt like it wanted to pull him into the hole. However, it grabbed the pouch of coins in David's shirt, then pulled with all its might, sending the coins flying into the hole. As the flame came higher, the tendril snuck back into the darkness. This time, not with laughter but what sounded like disappointment. David is regretful that he has lost his gift; however, more pressing matters have become important. He rolls onto his back, dodging the flame shooting out of the hole. The intensity of it lights everything around him; it does not look like a room David has been in this whole time. He cannot see a ceiling or walls; however, it has illuminated a door just behind David.

Wasting no time, he runs toward it, close behind the flame almost like a liquid begins spilling onto the floor. The space behind him begins to fill with fire. This is David's first time seeing this; as deadly and horrific as it is, it also appears quite strange. It is indeed fire, but it moves like water; the flames dance and flicker at the top, but slosh around below. Pulling himself out of his mesmerizing daze, David runs through the door. In an attempt to slow the flame, he pushes the door shut, hoping to slow it down by a second. As David climbs the stairs, he feels the heat behind him again. With no effort, the flame breaks down the door as if it is solely chasing after David with some feeling of vengeance. Waiting at the top, David comes to a room of five doors; not knowing which one to choose, he pick one at random. Coming to more stairs, David quickly groans out, "More?" under his breath. With no choice, he again climbs the stairs, only to get to a room with four doors now. "Oh, c'mon," David cries out as he again chooses another door at random. This pattern repeats, stairs to a room with three doors, more stairs to two doors. After this last set of stairs, the room only has one door; dragging himself through, it's the hallway to the exit. David is elated that he has finally come to salvation. However, the flame is close behind and David has barely been able to stay ahead of it. Finding any bit of energy he has, David heaves his body down the hallway. One step after another, the heat getting more and more intense, the light at the end shrinking and getting dimmer. As the fire nearly burns his backpack, David once again finds any strength he has, leaping for the exit. He can see nothing but darkness; he can feel his arms still wrapped around his head. However, he cannot see anything; fearing the worst, David began to wonder, Is this what death feels like? Soon, a familiar voice speaks up.

"Uh, David, you can open your eyes?" the voice was Sam.

Shocked, David opened his eyes, "Oh, I'm not dead."

Henry leans over him. "Welcome to the world of the living, David."

Ben simply reaches a hand out to help David up, humming happily.

"Thanks, Ben, I guess I closed my eyes; I was so scared," David tells the group as he stands back up.

"Well, if that wasn't the closest call we've all had," Anthony pats David on the back.

"Damn, Dave, why don't you try harder to scare us next time, huh?" Joseph exclaims while patting his head.

"Well, I have a story for you guys anyway, but first, can we get some food? I need to relax and eat," David tells the group.

CHAPTER 15

QUESTIONS

Placing the fork and knife down next to the plate on the table, David stares at the now-empty plate, content with finally having some food after a whole day. However, despite his stomach being full and happy, his face was not. David wore a sunken, saddened face, full of disappointment. Sitting around him, the group had gathered to listen to his story, as well as tell their own story of what happened to them.

Anthony starts off, "Well, it seems you had a hard time in there, huh, David? Either way, look at it like this, you're alive and that's more important."

"Yeah, Anthony makes a good point, David; it was just money," Sam consoles David, patting his head.

Looking around, David responds, "I know. I know, but they looked like the most expensive things I could have ever found. They could have given me the money; I need to end this all right now." David looks down at the plate once more, "And save Mom now."

Ben softly interjects, "Well, we'll just have to try harder next time."

Standing up, Anthony tries to give David hope, "We will do better next time, so don't feel so down; no one is disappointed in you; we're just glad you made it out."

Henry grumbles a little. "Well, I'm slightly disappointed."

Ben swiftly smacks the back of Henry's head.

Anthony continues, "Anyway, Joseph you got anything to say to David? Try and make him feel better."

Joseph, immersed in another housing pamphlet, looks up for a moment. "You're alive, that's more important; success comes and goes, we'll just try harder next time." Joseph looks back down and continues reading.

Both Sam and Ben sigh and shake their heads in unison; Sam mumbles. "I think you should try harder."

Anthony, trying to collect the group again to get on topic, says, "Anyway, we were in the middle of talking about our experiences to find anything similar or any clues about what's going on. So far, it seems we really haven't gotten far; we listened to David and his story. Now I say we keep going in the order of who came out of the abyss last. That means, before David came out . . . Henry, you came out just before him; what did you experience?"

Henry, scratching his chin like he's thinking, says, "Hmm, I remember it all like it was yesterday."

Sam stops him, "It was an hour ago."

"I just always wanted to say that." Henry continues, "Anyway, after I disappeared, I came to a set of red and gold doors. Unlike anything I've seen; they felt weird too; the red was soft like some kind of blanket or a sock."

"A sock?" Anthony asks.

Shrugging, Henry continues, "I don't know, it just felt weird. Anyway, I pushed open the two doors joined in the middle and walked through them. Inside was a large bright hall of some sort; it had glass cases all around. Some of these cases stood by themselves on pillars, just in the middle of the floor. Others were along the wall, but they were all roughly chest height, so I could look into them. So, clearly given the opportunity, I did, well, only a few; there were way too many to look at them all. But the ones I did look into were incredible; they all housed some kind of object. What these object did I don't know, but I do know they had to be valuable. Just about all of them were gold with gems in them, like jewelry; some even had swords like the one Joseph has now. But what's weirder is, there was even stuff like what David talked about in there. There were multiple men made of metal standing behind sets of glass; they were just standing there, didn't move or anything. I thought it was real weird, so instead of interacting with them, I just kept on moving. At the end of the hall was another door so I opened it and I got spit out back into the abyss by the exit. That's when I came out and met up with the rest of you who just got out."

"Well, that doesn't really answer anything now, does it?" Anthony remarks. "Ben, Sam, what happened to you two?"

Sam begins, "Well, me and Ben actually went to the same place. It felt kind of like our home, well, except that the buildings were much taller and more organized. We came out into an alleyway like one here, although slightly larger. It even had pipes on the buildings going up and down, some even into the ground. We decided to get out of the alleyway, and we came to a huge open section with even more buildings. They had lights on them all over the place and the people there were so many people, we felt like we couldn't breathe. Then even stranger, they had boats on land, the small ones had like one or two people in them as they moved around. Some even had a second floor with even more people on it; it was like a moving boat building. Everything seemed pretty incredible, and just like David, the people around us were speaking but we couldn't understand them. Not that it mattered; the people barely even acknowledged we existed; they all just kept moving, doing their own thing. However, the strangest is, Ben noticed some man in the crowd down the alleyway a little. The man looked straight at us and began walking toward us. We're not sure if they were friendly; he didn't look it, the way he was coming after us. So we ran in the other direction, and sure enough, the man was following us. I wish we weren't in a hurry; we missed so much cool stuff to see because of it, but no matter. We ran down an alleyway, jumped some kind of short wall that was there, and kept going. That man even jumped it too, like it was no problem. The only way we lost him was running through a door, then we bumped into some people. As we turned around, we found ourselves back in the abyss by the exit and we met Joseph and you, Anthony, waiting."

"So again, no answers, only questions; what could all this mean?" Anthony murmurs to himself as he sits down, thinking.

Henry leans in over the table, "So, Ant, what happened to you?"

"Not much," Anthony answers. "Like David, I found myself in a field, but it wasn't green. It was some kind of golden field; the grass was strange; it was tall, almost up to my waist; it flowed in the wind quite beautifully, however, like golden waves from the ocean or something. But overall, that was it; there were some noises in the distance, too faint to make anything of it. When I walked over a hill to look for them, I blinked and poof, I'm back in the abyss. Walking out of it, I found Joseph waiting; so, Joseph, that just leaves you; what happened?"

"Nothing," Joseph responds.

"Nothing? Nothing at all?" Sam asks.

"Yup, just showed up at the exit," Joseph responds nonchalantly.

Anthony begins speaking again, "So, then we really have nothing to go on. With everyone's experience being so different, there doesn't really seem to be any connection. Anyone has any ideas what this all could mean?"

Henry raises his hand, "I have one."

The group is shocked that Henry has one, so Anthony asks, "Okay, what is it, Henry?"

"I go home and get some sleep," Henry replies while standing up.

Everyone sighs deeply; Sam stands up as well. "Well, I didn't expect much, but I do agree; I am tired."

Anthony stand as well. "Then I guess some rest will do us all some good; but we should still think about our stories. Anything we could think of could be useful to understanding what is going on with us as of late."

Together, the rest of the group get up and head their own ways for the night; once again, they all go to sleep with more questions than answers.

CHAPTER 16

MOVING AROUND

Sitting on the couch, David is hunched over, rubbing the scab that formed over his knuckles. For a brief moment, he thinks about what had happened; in this moment, he fills with a little bit of pride— pride that he was an integral part of a plan to take down a giant beast. Furthermore, he came out more or less unscathed, nothing more than a thin line across his hand now, maybe some tired bones with it. In David's moment of thought, he is interrupted by his mother coughing. Half trying to just get his attention, the other half being a serious dry heaving cough. Looking up, David notices it's no longer just her legs that are solid stone. It's spread to her waist; she can barely bend from it now. With each passing day, it gets worse; every time it gets worse, David feels as if he's moving a step back from saving her. He questions why the rich who make the cure monopolize it, but he knows why; his question answers the harsh reality. If they didn't monopolize it, they wouldn't be rich in the first place. His only option is to play the game they have set up, in hopes of actually finishing it.

"Are you going to keep sitting there, looking at the holes in the floor-boards?" David's mother asks.

"I just feel stuck," David replies, sighing as he adjusts his posture.

"Ehh, don't we all? But it ain't like those holes in the floor can get you out of it," his mother says while shrugging her shoulders. "You just have to be like this damn rain, never stop moving," she continues while looking out the small porthole window.

"I guess, but it seems like Joseph took all my moving energy; it's only been a little over a week and he's already moved into a new home," David utters while he sits upright now.

"Then why not go see his new house? See what keeps him moving forward," his mother replies.

"I guess, I will, but this feels like familiar, however," David says while he stands up.

As David walks to leave the room, he looks back at his mother sitting there; his face sinks a little, wishing he could do more, do better. Nevertheless, he says goodbye, draping a raincoat over himself as he heads out into the rain. David, thinking about how to get to Joseph's new house, is very much intimidated. His previous home was only in District 54; however, he has made a leap to District 40 now. Even before David gets there, he has this uncanny feeling of unwontedness. For someone who has lived in District 57, just four district from the last, 40 already feels alien. But, perhaps this is nothing more than David's own self-doubt. To move his feelings elsewhere, David tries to think maybe the people and the atmosphere will be different. He thinks he should not judge a place he has not been to just yet, nor the people he has not met. With new-found confidence, David sets off for this new foreign land.

Stepping through the large metal gate labeled District 40, David feels compelled to lower his head, looking at nothing more than the ground. The very moment he crossed over, he could feel the uneasy eyes of the people. To David, this most certainly was a strange new land. The shops are mostly intact, save for a few cracks in the old walls here and there. The people are wearing clothing that match, as well as not full of holes or tattered. Then, their faces speak louder than anything, faces that say they are better, however, only by a small margin. So for the most part, the heavy atmosphere is left to silent stares and quiet judgement.

I'd rather have the feeling I might be mugged than this, David thinks to himself, walking down the street under this heavy feeling.

David shifts around the town quietly, dodging the rain drops along with any unnecessary attention. The only thing that gives him any sense of comfort is how wide the roads are. This extra space allows David to hide along the sides, moving as he needs too. One problem still arises; he has no direction of where to go, once again. Building up the courage, David decides to ask someone for some directions to Joseph's home. Just ahead of him, a man walks out of a shop and unfurls his umbrella, shielding him from the rain. With his free hand, he begins lighting the cigarette already in his mouth. Disrupting him, David quietly walks up to him politely, asking if he could help him find Joseph's address. Taking a puff of his cigarette, then holding it in his hand, the man replies, he never heard of the street address. Without another word, the man walks across the road, then down off to the side. David can only sigh, thinking to himself, Well, that was kind of expected. No matter how hard David tries, not one person is helpful; most disregard him entirely or just straight up refuse him.

Leaning against the wall of a building, David notices across the street a billboard on the wall, advertising homes for sale. It appears the owners of the advertisement have not taken it down in time. The advertised address of homes is where Joseph has moved to. David's luck has not run out just yet; the bottom of the billboard has an arrow pointing the way along with written directions below it. Well, at least the world is helping me, David thinks while memorizing the directions. Following the directions step by step, David soon arrives at Joseph's home; a larger, more held together apartment home sits. Surrounding his front steps, there's actual grass square plots; this small addition alone already sets David in awe. Walking up the four steps, David stands there on a small landing where he begins knocking on the door. After a moment, there's nothing, so David knocks again—still nothing. Thinking Joseph may not be home, David looks the building up and down; he even investigates the door and the frame of it. Just beside the handle, David notices a small button protruding from the wall. Intrigued, David presses it; faintly on the other side of the door, he hears bells being rung for a short moment, then they stop. Just as they stop, walking can be heard on the other side of the door. Step after step, the steps get closer and closer to the door. Soon, Joseph answers the door.

"Hello," Joseph looks around, then down at David. "Oh, hey, Dave."

"Hi, Joseph," David replies.

"So what can I do for you?" Joseph asks.

"I just wanted to come by and see your new home, is all really," David says.

"Oh, cool, come on in then; you're letting the rain in," Joseph says while turning around, entering his home.

"Thanks," David replies while entering, then closes the front door.

Instead of a hallway, David comes to the large room first, attached on the walls are the doors. Then off to the right side is the staircase going up. Looking around, David notices that the home is in quite a decent shape. The floor is levelled, not cracked or falling apart. The walls don't even have holes in them or any cracks. David can only find that the one flaw is some dirt that needs cleaning along with some chipped paint. Overall, the home is quite homely. David can tell that with some decent care, this would be the most held together home he would ever have. Interrupting David's gawking, Joseph speaks up.

"So you like it? It feels like it'll cost an arm and a leg, but if we keep diving and I can keep finding treasure like this, it's more than affordable," Joseph remarks while gesturing to the room.

"It sure is nice; a lot nicer than that last place you lived in. So you got any plans of moving again?" David asks, looking around.

"Nah, I kinda like it here," Joseph replies while sitting down on the couch. "It's nice and the district is kinda nice too, decent food and decent people".

"Yeah, decent," David mutters.

"You know, some of the other houses on the street are up for sale; I think it'd be kinda cool if you bought one and moved here too," Josephs says while pointing at David.

"I think I'm good, but besides that, if you're thinking of settling down here, then would you mind helping out?" David asks.

"Sure, what you need, Dave?" Joseph asks him back.

"Just help with Mom's cure fund; I've been putting everything I have into it, but it's not enough," David says.

Joseph's face sours ever so slightly; David continues, "I know you're busy with all this so you might not have time to give me the money. So whenever you do have time, my saving fund is locked away under the tree on the hill. Anytime you have spare money, it'd be a help if you just put some money in there."

Joseph's face lightens back up a little. "Sure, after the next dive, I'll put some money away for you."

"Thanks, Joseph, it means a lot; anyway, I shouldn't bother you anymore and it's getting late so I'm going to head home," David says while making his way to the front door.

"Alright, Dave, get home safe; I'll see you later," Joseph replies, waving him goodbye from the couch.

CHAPTER 17

SWORD TRAINING

Boarding the same boat on a different day, David makes his way to the island. This time for once, he has not gone there to go on a dive. David has other plans; during his last dive, he bore witness to a skill, real swordsman skill. Noticing his own weakness, David once again found himself in a position to make improvements. Stepping off the boat onto the familiar island, David spends a minute to find the only person who could train him. Soon, David stands still in the middle of some make-shift cobbled-together ring. Four wooden posts make a square, connecting them, two single pieces of rope tied together. Across from David stands the gate commander once again. Unlike last time, David came to him; he stands more composed, ready for what the commander has in store.

"So you want to learn how to swing your sword now?" the commander announces.

"Yes," David swiftly replies. The commander remains silent, looking down at David for some sort of answer. "Yes, sir," David says this time.

"Good, it's about time you put that rusty hand-me-down to some use," the commander says while pointing to the sword at David's side. "But why now all of a sudden?" he asks.

"I don't mean to be rude but I watched someone, someone with real sword skill; it was impressive really," David says excitedly, remembering watching the man in metal fight. "He swung the sword with real power, precision, and skill, almost like the sword was some kind of part of him."

Scratching his chin, the commander thinks for a moment. "Hmm, sounds like you met some kind of professionally trained swordsman. I don't think I could ever teach you to be as great as he is, but hey, I can get you to not die in the first sword clash."

"Thank you, I'll try my best." Another brief pause fills the air; the commander looks down at David as he did before. "Sir."

"Great, let's get you all bruised up," the commander shouts out with a hearty laugh.

Slightly concerned by the commander's words, David stares at him for a brief moment. This quiet moment is soon interrupted by the flat face of a sword slapping David in the face. Reacting too slow, David moves his hands to his face for defense after the sword has already attacked. Taking a step back, David looks up at the commander; his concern grows even more now. The commander brings the sword up to rest onto his shoulder, then begins talking.

"Listen well; here, we're going to start with the basics, and these basics aren't like you time doing physical training. First you need to get used to getting hit, flinching is not gonna help you. You have to see the attack and react accordingly. There's no preemptive dodging; if you move too early, I can change the direction of the attack. If you move too late, well, it's too late. Once you stop flinching, then we can get to work ironing you out. So, second, we'll work on dodging attacks. After that comes blocking, attacking, then countering attacks. But I'll tell you now, this ain't a fast process; learning to sword fight takes time. So how much time you got to learn?"

David, still rubbing his cheek, looks around for a moment, accessing his time. Finally, he lowers his hand, then looks up at the commander, "As much as I need."

The commander looks down at David, raising and eyebrow for a moment. Tilting his head back, the commander lets out another deep hearty laugh. The kind of laugh that comes straight from the gut. "Ha-ha, I like you even more now; let's get to it."

From morning to night that day, David trained relentlessly with the commander. Even after the suns set, David pushed himself to train, to a point that even scared the commander a little. Not only was David empowered by stamina and endurance but also his drive to learn as fast as possible. In the middle of the night, David stands beaten, covered in slight beads of his own blood and sweat. The sword armed, point forward; he's ready. His hands shaking, tired, bruised, and blistered. His legs wobbling like jelly, barely holding him up; David pushed to his limit and then some. Looking down at this zombie standing before him, the commander thinks briefly for a moment. Perhaps he should stop here to let the boy rest. This thought fades as the commander looks into David's eyes. Bright blue but light like a raging fire, David still stands so he can still fight. Chuckling to himself, the commander thinks how foolish his thoughts were to try and extinguish this blazing fight.

Now, even the commander readies his tired body for a fight once again, shouting, "Come at me."

David tenses up; hearing his battle cry, his hands become solid, his feet find their roots. He runs at the commander; the only sound to night filling the air is the clashing of metal.

CHAPTER 18

WAR

The light of the sun creeps up the land as it rises higher into the sky. As the wave of light makes its way over the island, it reaches David's face. Lying on his back in the dirt in front of the gate, he slowly opens his eyes as the light hits them. After a minute, he wakes up completely as the usual sound of six in the morning is rung out. Startled from his deep sleep, David shoots upward, sitting straight up and looking around. He brushes off the dirt and dust from his head, arms, then finally his body. He remembers last night, how his training drained him of all his energy. Too tired to even crawl, David fell, passed out where he sat. Rubbing his sore muscles, he thinks about how he didn't go home last night; his mother might be worried. But his thoughts soon disappear as the first to arrive at the gate is Joseph. Intrigued that David is here and sitting on the ground no less so early, Joseph asks him why. David explains that he had come for some sword training. He tells Joseph that it should be about time he learned how to use it. Joseph nods, then moves to the side of the gate, leaning against it. Not too soon, the mass of people begin filing into the gate, ready to dive. Wanting to get out of their way, David stumbles to his feet, then moves to the aide with Joseph. Finally reaching it, David falls back to the ground to rest while they wait for the others. Next to arrive is

Anthony, followed by Sam, then finally Henry. Curious, Anthony asks Sam where Ben is; she tells them he felt sick, so not to be a burden, he stayed home. Anthony's next curiosity is David, who looks quite beaten up, tired, and quite dirty. Wondering what David had been up to, Anthony asks him what he had done last night. Just like to Joseph, David explains he wished to be better at using his sword. He recounts his training last night with the commander. Surprised, Anthony applauds David for his conviction to learn how to fight. Henry comments that it looks more like the commander just beat him up, is all. Sam stretches her hand out to help David up, adding in that if he is too tired, he should rest today. Shrugging it off, David reassures her he is fine; he thinks to himself that he can't take a day off. The constant thought of not having the money yet, eats away at the back of David's mind every day. As David stands, he continues his response with the fact that he no longer has time to wait around. Sighing, Sam understands along with the rest of the group. However, she does emphasize on the fact that he should still look out for himself. Prepared, the group head into the abyss, ready to go on another dive.

Surprisingly, the first half of the dive goes very well. Together, they move from room to room, looking for valuables as they descend. Taking a moment to stop for lunch, they talk about how of all days for Ben to not come diving with them is a day when their dive is going well. When the conversations die down the group pack up their belongings, the ground below them shakes ever so slightly. Just enough for David to notice but it looks as if no one else has. With that, David decides to keep quiet, thinking he may still just be tired. Finding the next stairway down, they descend. As the group nears the door at the bottom, the ground shakes again, this time more violently. This last tremor was enough for the whole group to realize something has happened this time. For a second, they think of the oddity of the situation. They understand the monster has some control over the abyss. But this doesn't feel like control; this is quick and violent, yet no noise is heard with it. Before pressing on, the group call for a vote, a vote for whether they shall continue or turn back. Weighing their options, they know the moment they enter the abyss, their lives were in danger. So, together their conclusion is, what's a little bit more danger to an already dangerous situation? They'll never get to the bottom of all this mystery if they leave now. Henry thinks for a second, then blurts out, "What was the saying? Curiosity killed the cat." Looking back at him in place of Ben, Sam slaps the back of Henry's head, telling him to not say stuff like that. Regardless, they open the door and proceed through it, just like every other time before.

Walking through the door, Anthony expects a floor to be below him. However, there is a small drop; this forces Anthony to fall flat on his face into soft mud. Henry sticks his head through, looking around; as he looks down, he chuckles a little before jumping through. As Henry jumps down, his feet plant into the dirt; however, his knees give out, forcing him forward with his face into the mud as well. Next, Sam's head sticks out the door, laughing at Henry. Careful, Sam sits on the edge of the door, then steps down; Joseph and David follow after her. Looking around, the group notice wherever they ended up is just as dark as the abyss yet more dirty. Soon, the group hear a loud explosion far off into the distance. Despite the sound coming from so far away, the ground still shakes followed by small amounts of dirt falling from above. This commotion is met only with a small "huh" by Henry as he begins to stand up. Together, they look around for some way out of this dirt chamber. It doesn't take long for Sam to find a hallway dug out from the wall. Peering down the hallway another muffled explosion comes from the end of the hallway. This time, it was accompanied by a flash of light around a corner at the end of the hallway, along with the walls and roof shaking as small amounts of dirt rained down. The group look at each other in silent contemplation of what to do. Just a few seconds pass, then Anthony lets out a quiet "huh" this time. Leading the group, Anthony starts his way down the dirt corridor. Rounding the corner at the end, the familiar sound of rain can be heard. Just a few feet from the corner, the hallway comes to an end, opening up. However, only the top is open; both side stretch up to just about head height. Anthony observes their surroundings, noticing the puddles that have gathered. Along with the consistent rain, the walls have marks on them; this confirms the fact that someone dug this.

Anthony stands fully straight to get a look over the trench they're in. With his whole head exposed, he turns to one side, then to the other. Nothing but craters in the ground, and broken, burned, and dead trees scattered around. The base of the trees suggest, this was a forest; however, it no longer houses any living plant. Suddenly, a loud crack passes right next to Anthony's head; just behind him, some dirt is kicked into the air. Trailing behind, a bang follows soon after the crack. However, by instinct, Anthony ducks back down into the trench; as he does, he lets out a surprised "woah." Rubbing the inside of his ears with the tips of his fingers, he tells the group not to stand up apparently. They're hunched over to ensure their heads don't go over the wall. The group talk about what that was just now; however, never being here or experiencing anything like this, they have no idea. One thing they do think of is that if someone or something went through the trouble of attacking, perhaps it was only defending something. Just maybe it was something valuable, something very valuable. Not knowing where or how that enemy attacked is quite the challenge, so their plan is to not be seen at all. As the group stays low in the trench, they follow along it, hoping it leads to a treasure of some sort. All they find for a short time is nothing more than slight turns, bends, and straightaways. The whole time they are moving, the air is filled with occasional sounds of explosions in the distance. Along with these explosions, smaller bangs follow after; none of these come close to the volume of the one from before. The quantity of bangs and explosions get louder and increase in number. Soon, the group reaches the end of the trench; here, it slopes up like a ramp, just at the edge of a beaten forest. This forest appears to still have some life in it for now; only a handful of trees still live. As they survey where to go, the flash of explosions lights up the forest coming from the other end of it. Deciding its best to move fast, Anthony sprints into the forest, hiding behind a tree. Waiting, as the group doesn't hear a loud crack, Henry runs out next to Anthony. Again nothing; determining it's safe, the other three run into the forest. Carefully, they walk over tree trunks toppled over, roots jutting out from the mud. The explosions getting louder as well as the smaller bangs and the cracking noise too. Faint but loud enough to make everyone look around worried.

Suddenly, the branch right next to Henry shatters apart, followed by the cracking noise. Confused, the group hunch over again to bring their heads down. More cracking falls onto the group, the trees shattering and breaking. The group scatter, not knowing what to do but taking cover behind whichever trees will hide them. David falls into one of the large craters; being careful, he stands, shouting for the group to come to him. Sprinting, they make their way to the hole; Joseph along with Henry dive in. Anthony helps Sam and both slide their way down. The moment they get under the ridge, the bangs and cracking stop. A moment to breathe, they make sure no one was hurt; so far everyone is good. Another explosion lights the crater like it was daytime; this brief moment illuminates two random men the group didn't notice. Looking over in shock, Anthony, along with Joseph, stand up to unsheathe their swords ready. Trying to calm the two down, the two men lying there wave their hands, showing they are not threatening the group as well as trying to tell them to lie back down. Just as the warning happens, the cracks and bangs return, forcing the two back down into the dirt. The other two men look to be relieved after the bangs stop; then they begin talking to the group. However, just as before, they cannot understand each other. The men realize this as well; one of them pushes up his glasses back to his eyes to look into a pocket of his jacket. He pulls out a small pad with a pencil, then draws. His doodle is crude and squiggly using only stick figures, but it gets the point across. On one side, he drew himself his friend and the group in the forest. Opposite them, on the other side, is a group of people who he drew like him; they must be friends. However, he points out a line of stick figures who he drew look evil and angry between the two men and their friends. The group realizes the two men have been separated from their friends, with a group of bad people in the way. The group talk amongst themselves for a minute, deciding what they should do.

David speaks first, "I think we should help them."

"And what would we get out of it?" Henry asks.

"I don't know, maybe we get to live, Henry," Sam retorts.

Henry scoffs, "I could take them."

"In what? A who's going to die first competition?" Anthony chuckles.

"Hey, I don't have this sword for nothing, you know," Henry says as he points to the sword.

Joseph gets between them, "Look, we're getting off track here; if we help them, maybe they'll reward us."

Henry looks over in contemplation. "That wouldn't hurt," he murmurs.

"So, we agree we help them, then they might help us?" David asks everyone.

The group look at each other silently, nodding in agreement. David, acting as some sort of mediator, gives the two men a thumbs up of approval. The two men raise one eyebrow, then look at each other; they believe they understand. Regardless, they nod in approval to each other, then begin some kind of plan. The two talk as the group stares at them in confusion; the men point, wave their hands, and get loud with each other. Someone would think this is an argument rather than a brainstorming session for a plan. Despite the small argument, the two have calmed down and come to an agreement. The one with the glasses tears the paper with the drawing out of the little book. Flipping to a new page, he begins drawing once again. Using the same crude stick drawings like before, he shows them all in the hole they're sitting in. Then, he points to his friend on the paper; he uses his finger to trace along to a new hole. Pointing back to the group, he points them, including himself, into the other direction. Then when he gets to the side of the enemies, he points to them, fighting. Understanding, David makes sure the group knows the one man will act as a distraction. When their enemies are distracted, they, along with the other man, will ambush them from the side. Everyone nods, agreeing on the plan although skeptical; the group have no other alternative.

Getting himself ready, the other man talks to himself, bobbing up and down for a moment, then grabs the long object next to him. It's long and made of wood with metal bits on one side. As he stands up, out of the hole, he brings one side up to his shoulder. Pulling some small metal bit with his finger, the other end lets out the loudest bang the group has heard. Light flashes illuminate them all for a brief second. Then the cracking sound is heard; dirt kicks up around them, trees shatter again. The man runs to the side, yelling and letting out more bangs from the object in his hands. David does not fully understand how but knows enough to grasp a general idea of what has been happening. As they wait for the man with glasses to move, David has an idea. He tells the group his idea, which is, those bangs and cracks are made by the enemies using that strange object. Theorizing, Anthony suggests they may be long range weapons, but this is where their understanding ends. At the very least, they all have some small nugget of information. Listening for a moment, finally the man waves his hand for the group to follow him. Jumping up out the hole, the man uses his weapon toward the enemies as the group run. The group dive into a new hole; the man follows soon after. Ducking down, he listens again; the bangs continue from a distance. Standing, he urges the group to follow again; this time, he doesn't use the weapon, just leads the group around. In the darkness, it's difficult to follow but they manage until suddenly he disappears. Looking around, Anthony brings up his light; finding another trench, he jumps in; following his lead, the others jump in as well. Crouched down, he brings one finger to his mouth, telling the group to be quiet. Leading them down the trench, they walk through puddles of mud and those weapons being used, next to the occasional dead body. The man sneaks down the trench until the enemies' attacks get louder. David, Henry, Anthony, Sam, and Joseph ready their swords; they sneak closer as the enemies are still distracted. Right next to them, they hide in the darkness; however, soon the dim light of their lanterns give them away to one enemy. He turns to face them; however, before being able to do anything, the man with the glasses uses his weapon. It's a quick succession of a bang, a loud crack, that passes the group, then ends in a ping as the enemy falls to the ground. A small hole has appeared in the helmet of the man; this causes a pause in the enemies, as they now all turn. It's too late; the group each target an enemy, thrusting their swords, taking one down. Behind them, the man covers them to the side, the other man leaning against a tree begins using his weapon. The enemies are surrounded, being attacked from all angles, disorganized and disoriented. Quickly, the enemies are cut down both in number and literally. As the skirmish dies down, no more enemies remain; the man that acted as a distraction joins up with the rest, safe and sound.

Regrouped, the two men shake hands, most likely congratulating them on a successful fight. Now that everything has calmed down, the two begin talking. Since the group cannot understand them, they take this time to look around. Joseph picks up one of the weapons, spinning it, looking it over. Henry searches the bodies, pretending to check if they're dead; in truth, he's looking for anything valuable. Anthony regularly checks over the trench walls on lookout, making sure they stay safe. David, kneeling down, lifts up one of the enemies' helmets, looking them face to face. It's nothing more than another man; by his appearance, he's around Joseph's age. Reflecting, David thinks, he's fought the darkness in the abyss, even fought a towering monster. But never a man, another human; he knows so far they have tried to kill him, given the chance. However, the only question he asks is why; the monsters were a fight for survival. People fighting people never really occurred to David as a possibility. In his moment of silence, Sam pats David on the shoulder, asking what he was doing. Thinking, he replies as he stands up, then walks over to rejoin the group. Henry has collected some bits of metals; being slightly courteous, he disperses some to the others. During this exchange, the two men approach the group. The one with glasses has one small bag in the palm of each hand; one he hands to the group. Anthony takes it; opening it, reveals coins both gold and silver. It's a reward for helping them; the other bag seems to come with a catch of sorts. Holding up another drawing the man with the glasses points to a huge expanse of open land on the other side of the land their friends. Then he holds the other bag up; if they help them continue, the group gets the other bag. Noticing the great value of the first reward, the group unanimously agrees to help. Their only problem is, the middle comes off as a mystery; the man left it vague as to what is there. Or even the two don't know what is between them. However, the amount of money they have a potential of making, makes it all worth to them.

Keeping in line with using the cover of night, they make their way over the trench wall, into the destroyed forest. The occasional flash of explosions light their way forward. The sounds of battle get closer as they creep through the forest with great caution. Between the explosions, bangs, and general sounds of battle, David hears something that pierces all that noise, something strangely familiar; as they move, the sound grows. David has heard this before, but in the current situation, he can't quite make out what it is. Soon, even without the explosions, the ground itself starts to rumble on its own. A new sound joins the others; a deep thud explosion just before a louder explosion. Closer now, the familiar sound can be made out; it's mechanical; the sound reminds David of his old work. The sound of gears turning, pistons racing, metal clanging against metal. Thinking they are coming up to a factory, David soon realizes how wrong he is. As they reach the edge of the forest, an open plain of fighting plays out before them. Sprawling trenches, men using their weapons toward each other, craters litter the land. Up on a small hill, they see the machine lumbering around, letting out hails of fire from one end of it. Without even knowing what this machine is, David, along with the group, can tell just by the fear it gives off, that it's dangerous. Standing before them, the machine is square with rounded edges. It's a towering behemoth, two people tall, twice as long; sitting on top of the square is a rounded half circle, rotating every now and then. Protruding from the circle is a short fat cylinder that bursts with fire, letting out a projectile. The projectile is slow enough to see for a brief second but fast enough to travel a distance. Where this projectile lands, leaving nothing but devastation as it explodes on impact. The sides of it spark as the men use their tiny weapons in comparison. Leaving nothing but a scratch, from the outside, this thing cannot be stopped. Yet the two men point the group toward it—this mechanical beast is the objective. Shocked, the group look at the two in stunned disbelief. They have to attack that, that invincible mechanical beast? Where to begin, feels like an insurmountable question. However, the two men look confident in the group. Again, the man in glasses holds up a doodle of the machine; he points to the top of the square. It appears, on top is a hatch of sorts that he shows them. Next, he reaches for his bag, pulls out a small square with wires attached to a switch. His drawing shows he wants someone to get to the machine. Once there, flip the switch, throw the square into the hatch, then get away. The plan is simple; the execution, however, is far from easy.

"So, who wants to do it?" Anthony asks the group. Everyone looks at each other, then back to Anthony.

"What?" Henry asks.

"What do you mean, what? I asked who wants to do it," Anthony replies.

"Well, I think we all sort of expected you to do it as the leader of the group and all," Sam says.

Pointing to the machine, Anthony replies. "That thing is terrifying; I don't want to do it."

David pats Anthony's shoulder, "I believe in you, leader."

Anthony swipes away David's hand, "Look, fine, let's vote; who do you all think has the best possibility of achieving this?"

Unanimously, everyone points to Anthony. "I don't know what I expected from that," Anthony grumbles. "Fine, I'll lead the charge, but I'm not going alone; the more people, the better."

Again, the group look at each other, then back at Anthony. "I guess we all have to earn that money somehow," David says.

Agreed now, Anthony will be the spearhead of this while the others follow behind. Anthony takes the square from the man; for a minute, he inspects it, being mindful of the switch. In the drawing, the man made it clear to only flip it when they get close. All together, they observe the battle-field; luckily, they have come from the side. Unluckily ,they're closer to the side of the enemies. Waiting, looking, listening, they want the best possible chance of success. After the machine fires, their chance is now, while it and the men around it are distracted. They sprint together in a line. Dodging broken trees, leaping over rocks, and holes, they do their best to stay low to avoid detection. Getting closer, one man in a trench turns, looking at the group. He yells out; the others turn to look. From behind the group, the two men use their weapons, causing a commotion along with taking out a man or two. The enemies duck down to avoid being hit. As they inch closer to the machine, a small hole opens on the side. A cylinder juts outs and the rapid bangs begin. Dirt flies up as it misses; it takes a moment for it to get its bearings. Soon it hits its mark. One straight into Anthony's calf, another in his thigh. The small projectiles make a line up his torso, stopping him where he stands. As he kneels on the ground, his clothes begin to turn crimson red. In one final moment, he flings the box toward David, who's the furthest ahead. Everyone pauses, coming to a halt, looking back. Henry cries out, "NO." Sam takes a step toward Anthony, but he waves her and the group off. David picks up the square, meeting eyes with Anthony. One look shared between them tells David everything he needs. He turns back, sprinting again at the machine. Henry jumps into the closest trench, pick-ing up a weapon from a dead enemy. He shoulders it like he saw the two men do, then pulls the trigger. The projectile pings off the machine. The force of the weapon is unlike anything he's experienced. His shoulder feels broken but he grits his teeth. He uses it time and time again, causing the small cylinder to start pointing at him, ignoring David. It fires at Henry, hitting dirt as he ducks down. As he comes down the trench, a man swings a blade at the end of the weapon down at Henry. It's blocked by Joseph's sword; he kicks the middle of the weapon out of his hands, giving him the opening to thrust his sword up through the enemy. During Henry's distraction, David made his way to the side wall of the machine. The sound of an engine whirring to life, the machine starts to move backwards. David has to jog with it to stay out of enemy fire. Frantically, he looks for some way up, something to grab. He finds a small handle and grabs it with all his force. Attached to the machine, David begins climbing it. Providing more distraction, Henry picks up another weapon after the last stopped functioning. He fires it again; the machine fires back; Henry ducks down. Joseph provides cover in the trench, holding enemies back. In the back, an enemy throws something at them. It misses Joseph, bounces off a wall, then rolls to Henry's side as he lying down in the trench. Quickly, Henry looks at it confused, then looks up at Joseph. A deafening explosion between the two sends Joseph to his back. The dirt in the air settles and Joseph sitting up looks down at Henry, who's unresponsive and bleeding from head to toe, with shrapnel embedded into every part of him. With no time to process everything and still disoriented, Joseph is attacked. Joseph blocks another blade wielded from another man standing over him, Joseph is forced back to continue the fight in the close quarters. On top of the machine, David finds the hatch; looking at it, he has no idea how to open it. After a brief second, it unlatches and then opens and a man pops up. In his hand is a small weapon; he swings it around to try to hit David. David falls back, sitting down; the man points the weapon at David. Knowing it's nothing good, David kicks it back and up, forcing the top part to hit the man in the face. This opening allows David to flip the switch. Bringing it up, he hurls it down, hitting the man again, then dropping it in the opening the man is standing in. Concerned, the man looks down, then just before he could panic, David grabs hold of the hatch. Nearly standing on it, David manages to force it down along with the man. David's hand was on some lever on the outside; he turns it, forcing the hatch closed. Objective complete, David rolls off the machine; landing on his hands and knees, he crawls away as fast as he can. Getting only a small distance away, the machine bursts into flames from the inside. Fire shoots out from any hole it can find. Its engine dies down as the back end of the machine explodes. The behemoth is killed.

For a brief moment silence takes over the field. No weapons being fired, no explosions, not even a yell. Soon, multiple whistles come from the other side of the battle. The people they helped begin rushing from the trenches. Joseph, still fighting an enemy, notices that they begin to panic. Deciding to run, the enemy throws its weapon at Joseph as a way to escape. They all start fleeing from their trenches. The allies dispatch any remaining enemy taking over the trenches, driving them all away. Taking a moment, David rolls over to see the one-sided fight now. The man in glasses appears over David, offering to help him up. The two make their way to Sam who's kneeling over Anthony, with tears streaming down her face. David's eyes begin to tear up as well looking down at his friend. Joseph, standing in the trench still, calls David over. Henry is lying in the mud in between other bodies as well. For some reason, he sticks out the most, despite being just as dirty and bloody. David, looking down, asks Joseph what now. Joseph kneels down, collecting the valuables Henry had taken. Standing back up, he wipes his face and tells David to collect their reward; then they'll find a way back.

"What about them?" David asks.

"They're lost," Joseph replies as he climbs out of the trench.

Turning around, the man with glasses hands David the other bag. Understanding their sacrifice, he doesn't hand it to them with any joy. David puts it away into his backpack, then the two collect Sam who's still crying by Anthony's body. Joseph and David help her to her feet; slowly and silently, they walk back into the forest. Now that the sound of fighting has come to a halt, nothing but their surroundings can be heard. Their footsteps splashing in puddles of mud. Solitary birds chirp here and there in the distance. Peace has come over the land, but not for the people walking on it. Coming back to the first hole they found the two men, standing there alone in the hole a familiar, ominous black closed door. Opening it, they find themselves at the beginning of the abyss, in the first long hallway. After not too long, they exit the gate, back home. Stunned, David asks, why of all times, this was the easiest getting home. Silently, Joseph thinks; his conclusion is, they made a trade.

"A bad trade," David responds. Joseph can only agree in silence.

CHAPTER 19

THE LAST HOME

David is home, sitting on the couch, doing nothing but counting the cracks on the ceiling. For a brief moment in time, not a single thought enters David's mind. However, he is brought back to reality by the realization that his main goal is still not achieved. Despite the almost million dollars he has gained, the cure for his mother is still just out of reach. "Why must something be so expensive?" curses David. Nonetheless, he has to do something; he's come too far to quit. Davids contemplating about life was interrupted by his mother asking him a question.

"Can you bring this flower and vase to Joseph's home?" David's mother asks.

"I don't really feel like moving or going to his house right now, Mom," David replies.

"I know you're tired and there was an accident at work, but if you sit around like that, you'll end up like me." His mother raises her arms from her blanket. The disease has progressed to her fingers becoming stone solid.

"I know, I know, I just," David looks down; his eyes begin welling up.

"It's hard losing a friend; I felt the same when your father passed. I just want to encourage you to do more, to be better." His mother stops him.

"Yeah, I'll dig around, find the strength;" David says while wiping his eyes.

"That's my son; I know how strong you are, just like me." His mother does a feeble attempt of flexing her arms.

David chuckles just the slightest. "Yeah, okay, Mom, I'll be back then." David stands up and stretches backwards. Straightening out, he walks over to the table where the flower in the vase sits.

It's a strange blue color; its petals are wrapped in between each other in multiple layers. The stem holding it up is thin but sturdy with two leaves on either side. The vase holding the flower is simple in design: a square bottom that slowly tapers to a circle at the top. The width of the opening is the size of the palm of David's hand. It's not quite tall, however; just barely half the length of David's forearm. David picks it up, inspecting it.

"How did you get this?" David asks.

"I got the neighbor to go down and buy them both for me; after all, you two are so busy nowadays," his mother replies.

"Right, sorry, I'll see about getting Joseph to come visit," David says as he heads for the door.

"Mmm, that would be nice," the last thing David hears his mother say as he leaves.

Looking through a small gap between the buildings, David can see the other side of the island. District 9: it's a long way around the island.

Spending the first half of the morning walking to Joseph's house, David has had quite the adventure. The neighborhoods got more fancy, the streets are wider, the people, more distant. Coming to a closed metal gate, David is halted by guards. Two large muscular men in black dress suits stand before him. Access to District 10 to 1 is restricted to property owners and family. David explains that his brother had just purchased a house in District 9 and, he would like to visit. One of the guards holds up a clipboard with paper on it. He flips over a few pages, then asks David for his full name. After David tells the man, he flips another page, writes something down, then moves out of the way. The two men open the gate for David to pass through; as he does, they quickly shut it behind him. Walking down the wide streets of District 10, David feels eerily alone. Despite being and feeling out of place in the other districts, this just feels abandoned. Along with the lack of people, the homes feel just as lonely. Each stand completely alone, surrounded by their own green grass, trees, and water fountains. One of the few people David encounters is a man trimming a tree in a yard. He doesn't acknowledge David at all but keeps on diligently working. Quickly, David made his way to District 9. Here, it's just as silent as 10; the only sounds are the birds flowing water and the wind. Had it not been so abandoned, David might have found it peaceful. Finally, he ends his walk at the large front steps of Joseph's home. Pristine marble with gold inlays and large pillars hold up an overhang over the front of the doorway. As he looks over the door, he sees it's a dark red wood with a silver knocker in the direct center. Not seeing a button like the last house, David decides to grab the loose part of the door knocker. Bringing it up, then down a few times, the sound penetrates the whole house. This time, there is no sound of footsteps; suddenly the door cracks open, then slowly creaks open. Joseph stands there in new fancy clothes; his shirt still has a price tag on the sleeve. He greets David slightly coldly.

"Oh, Dave, what can I do for you?" Joseph starts.

"Mom wanted me to bring you this; it's a house-warming gift," David says while holding the flower out.

"Thanks," the only thing Joseph says while taking the flower. "So you want to come in?" he continues.

"Sure," David replies.

For David, walking into the large house is just as impressive as the outside. The landing in front of the door is quite large. Before stepping up, Joseph tells David to take his shoes off and to leave them by the door. After doing so, David steps up into the large open room. Directly in the center is a wide set of stairs leading upwards to the second floor. Joseph explains that's where his bedroom is. Walking over to the right, they enter another room, the kitchen; David is surprised to see a whole room just for the kitchen. To the left of the kitchen, behind the stairs and spanning the whole house is the living room with couches, separate seats, tables, even a decorative dresser in the corner. Going left again, they enter another room, a library of sorts, with empty bookshelves and desks. Left again, they find themselves back at the beginning; the rooms make one giant loop around the stairs. Impressed, David asks to see the second floor; Joseph excessively denies, implying that it is personal and that he would not like anyone disturbing anything. Concerned but accepting that Joseph deserves his own space, David leaves the matter aside. Joseph, while pointing out small details in the architecture, is slowly corralling David toward the door. Getting there, Joseph finally stops and asks if David has any more questions. Looking up, David asks two things: when Joseph will visit their mother. The second being, what will they do about diving, now that Anthony and Henry are gone. Joseph assures David he will take over as the leader and that the four of them are more than enough to dive. As for visiting his mother, his only response is, soon. David walks out the door saying his goodbye; Joseph quickly does the same as he closes the door. Turning around, David looks out at the island; a slight breeze hits his face. He takes a deep breath in, then lets out just as deep of a sigh.

CHAPTER 20

SAND

A few days have gone by after Anthony's and Henry's passing. Joseph, David, Sam, and Ben have met up outside the gate. For the past few times they met, they never felt like going in for another dive. To ruin their mood further, it has not even rained scince the pairs passing. The sun continues to shine, and the world still turns without a care. Lying in the dirt, David, Sam, and Ben look up at the blue sky.

"This doesn't feel right. It always rains; why not now? It feels like something, I don't know," David sighs.

"It's just wrong, like we should be sad, but the weather makes it hard to," Sam continues David's thought.

Quietly, Ben lets out a deep hum of agreement.

"I'm not even sure I want to keep diving anymore," Sam says. "Maybe with the money I have, I could start a store or something," she continues.

"That'd be nice; I could help if you'd like," Ben says.

"Hm, that would be kind of nice, Ben," Sam replies.

"I'm not going to stop you, but I say we at least go on one more dive before stopping," Joseph interrupts.

"Just one last one?" David asks.

"Yeah, just one," Joseph replies.

Thinking for a moment, David does the math in his head. Before coming here, he had taken inventory of the money he had saved. If they could successfully do one more big dive, David will have enough money to save his mother. That is, if they survive it.

"Fine, one more time, but no matter the money, we prioritize living instead of a reward this time," David says while sitting up.

"Yeah, having more capital for starting a store would help, so just one more time," Sam agrees.

"Hmm, if everyone agrees, then I'll go for one last time as well," Ben quietly murmurs.

Standing up, the three collect their bags along with any other belongings. They ready themselves for what will be their final adventure together. Joseph takes the lead with the three trailing behind him. Just like all the others, nothing of note happens in the beginning, just rooms of strange, burned objects and structures. Valuables scattered in dark corners, a door into a room, a staircase down into another room. The group wishes this had been their normal experience every time. Nothing more than a simple get in, then out, along with occasional close encounters with the monster—but overall, nothing that no one else has ever experienced. Ever since the beginning, they did always wonder what made them special. 10:47: the last time David had taken note of before entering a new door at the bottom of a staircase. As the door opens, a familiar sense of trouble washes over them all.

Wind bursts out from the door violently, forcing it fully open. The power behind the wind is strong enough to make the group stagger. Deafened by the wind, before they could realize, they find the wind carried sand with it. Thick and blinding, the sand attacks them. Brushing exposed skin, it feels like small razors. Deafened, blinded, and confused, they stretched their arms out, trying to find each other. Barely able to see his own nose, David grabs hold of a cloth in front of him. Doing his best to shield his eyes with his free hand, he tries yelling out. His attempts are useless; David can hardly hear his own thoughts; no one around him would be able to hear him. Taking step after step, David finds it increasingly hard to walk. The ground is no longer solid; as his foot comes down, it compresses into the ground, shifting, moving; it's as if the ground itself is trying to eat him. As the darkness fades, light begins to shine. The wind fades slowly, the torrent of sand settles. Standing in the middle of nowhere, mountains of sand surround him. Surveying the land, David looks over to the cloth he clung to. It's worn by a corpse of a human, rotten flesh, with every hole spilling sand. David lets out a small surprised "Ew," before letting go. Clearly, the age of the corpse suggests it's no one from the group; this relieves David slightly. Looking around, he appears to be alone, along with being in some kind of hole. Digging his feet out of the sand, David stands up. As he does, Ben sits up from underneath the sand on the hill to his side. He spits out sand and is trying to get it off his face. David asks if he knows where anyone is. Getting up from his burial, he points down where he sat. A hand digs out, following behind it, Sam's head pops out of the sand. She looks up at Ben, then comments that he's quite heavy. Apologizing, Ben reaches down to help pull Sam out of the ground. Together again, David asks them if they know where Joseph is located now. The two can only shrug. Thinking he must be close by, David climbs his way up the dune to get a better advantage point. Higher up now, David can see nothing but sand, sand, and more sand. Reaching up next to him, Sam asks where they should go now. "I don't know," the only words that could possibly enter David's mind. Where could they even go? There are no buildings, no landmarks, nothing. Faintly carried by the wind, they could hear someone yell out for somebody. Hiking up another dune, they come across some half-buried structure jutting from the sand. There are all kinds of pipes, sheet metal, and random rusted-away metal. All the while, dangling from the top, Joseph is caught by the back of his shirt. Noticing the three of them in the distance, he angrily yells to get him down. Relieved he's alive, they laugh for a moment before venturing up to unhook him.

All together now, Joseph asks if they have seen or found anything of interest. Sam holds up a pile of sand, asking if this will fetch a high price. Joseph only mocks the comment, saying if it did, they're the richest people ever. Thinking, the group try to come up with some plan or at the very least, a direction to march in. Soon, their answer comes to them; off in the distance, over a dune, there's an explosion. Following the explosion, smoke begins billowing up into the sky to mark their way forward. Turning to each other, their only way toward anything appears to be danger once again. Taking every measure to be cautious the group peek over each dune, before moving forward. After just a handful of dunes, they reach the source of the explosion: a small wooden town, making two little rows of buildings, some more held together than others. Most noticeable is the large one currently on fire. Surrounding it are people who are in panic, rushing back and forth, with some carrying buckets of water to the building. A select few, however, are climbing onto some mechanical looking animal. It stands on four legs, and as soon as the rider gets on, they gallop away into the sands. The only thing they can recognize, but which are still different, are the weapons they're holding. They appear different in nature but have the similar feeling and look to them. Just outside of the town, moving away is a carriage being towed by two of those machine animals. The people leaving the town appear to be chasing the carriage. If there was a fight that caused the explosion, it has moved on now. Surveying the town, Joseph comes up with an idea.

"Let's take advantage of this mess," Joseph says to the group.

"What are we going to steal? More planks from one of those buildings?" David comments.

"I know, that's the thing; look at all of them. See anything strange?" Joseph points toward the town.

"Besides the fact that this is a town surrounded by sand inside of the abyss?" Sam replies.

"Not that; look at them specifically; how some are different from others; anything stand out?" Joseph asks again.

David stares intently at the buildings, looking each one over again and again. After his second pass over, he indeed notices something strange about one building in the middle. "Is it that one, the brick one with metal bars on the windows?"

"Yes, why is that one brick and not wood and what's with the bars?" Joseph exclaims.

"So you think that building has something of value in it?" Sam asks.

"Most likely; so this chaos provides the perfect cover; they'll be too confused to notice us sneak in, then out. Plus, the men with the weapons have already left. So its low risk, which makes it no harm in checking out. We only have something to gain from it," Joseph explains.

"I hate to admit it, but Joseph has a good point about all this; what about you two?" David says.

"As long as the risk stays low, I'm fine with this," Sam states; Ben nods in agreement.

"Great, let's get rich and put an end to all this; we'll move when I say," Joseph asserts.

Watching the townsfolk, Joseph waits for the best moment to insert themselves. After a brief time passes, he leaps down the dune, waving them to follow him. Together, they rush down across an open section, finally making it to the rear of a building. Peering through the window, they find a family has gathered in the room. The group is not able to understand what they are saying; they most likely are talking about the recent explosion. In the corner, a mother is comforting her crying infant. Crouching down below the window, Joseph gestures for them to keep quiet. They sneak along the wall to the corner of the home. Joseph peers around the corner, down the alley, between the two buildings. He can see people running around still in chaos. Not letting the opportunity go to waste, they walk down the alley to the main street, stopping to use the shadow of the building to hide them from the sunlight. Keeping track of the busy street, Joseph waits for there to be the least amount of people. After a group pours water onto the building engulfed in flames, they return to fill them with water again. This gap allows the group to move behind their backs across the street. Gathering at the door, Joseph tries to open it, but it remains tightly shut. Ben gets them to clear the way of the door; cracking his knuckles, he prepares himself. With the little distance in front of the door, Ben barges into the door, forcing the lock to break, opening it. David last inside attempts to close the door, however because Ben has broken it David can only close the door enought to leave a small crack in the door, making the door appear it has been closed. Looking around, they find it's nothing more than an empty room with a window cut out of the wall in front of them. "More security," Joseph groans; to the right is another door. The group look over to Ben, encouraging him to do it again. As he rams the second door, it comes off at the hinges, causing Ben to fall. As Ben kneels to get up, he rubs his shoulder, looking up. In front of him and the group, a large man is towering over the already tall Ben. A thick bushy mustache sits on his lip, spilling over to fall down to chin. A scar runs up his cheek over his right eye.

Sam whispers to David, "Is this the monster you fought with the metal man?"

David replies, "No, but he's close to it."

Looking behind him is a room. Joseph tells them, he must be guarding the room. Given the short length of the building, that must be the last room. That must be where they could find any valuables.

"I don't think our friend here is going to let us take it Joseph; now what?" asks David.

"Sam, Ben, you get to the room; me and David will keep this guy busy," Joseph announces.

Simultaneously, Sam and Ben choose a side to run on next to the man. Ben chose the left of the man, so Sam goes to the right. He leans over with his left arm to grab Ben; however, Joseph stops him, grabbing his arm. With his right hand, the man swings, punching Joseph in the face, knocking him back, freeing his arm. David drawing his sword, lunges at the man ready to impale the man in the chest. In one swing of his arm the man connects with Davids sword with a trumendious amount of force, so much so Davids sword is sent flying accross the room implaing the wooden wall. David, mostly confused that a man just did this, soon finds himself on the floor as the man shoves David away. Taking this moment, Joseph draws his own sword, while charging at the man. Joseph raises his sword up as high as he can, the swiftly brings it down towards the man. One simple turn, the man dodges Josephs sword, as Josephs sword clashes agaisnst the ground, the man raises his foot up then steps down on the sword, forcing it out of Josephs hand. With the sword under the mans boot, he kicks the sword away behind him as it slides across the floor to the other side of the room, away from them all. Joseph, equally confused as David was before, is soon punched in the face unexpectedly. Coming in, David punches up into the man's exposed side. He tilts his head over, looking more angry than before. Twisting his torso, he swings his right elbow around. David ducks under; however, his left fist follows suit, connecting to David's side, pushing him to the ground. Joseph punches the man's left side ribs, then shakes his own hand in pain for a minute. During this, the man lifts his left knee, then extends his foot out, kicking Joseph in the gut. Lying on the floor still, David kicks his right leg behind the knee. Davids kick brings the man down to his knee. Joseph comes back with his own kick to the man's face. He tilts his head to the left, letting Joseph's foot pass by his head. The man rests Josephs right knee on his shoulder as the man grabs Josephs left foot. Easily, the man lifts Joseph, throwing him over his shoulder. As Joseph lands on the ground, David lands a punch across the man's face. The man swings wide with his right arm forcing David to take a step back to avoid it. Spinning on his right knee, the man swings his left foot over, moving both of David's legs out from under him. David, looking up, sees only a fist coming, landing another punch. After the first one, the man lifts his arm back, ready to swing again. Joseph quickly rushes in, running into the man, attempting to tackle him. However, the man barely moves at all. Not quitting yet, Joseph is trying to squirm his way around to choke the man. As the two toss and turn, David kneels back up and lands a punch to the mans face. Wrestling one person is a hassle but two becomes a problem. Joseph finally gets his arms around the man's neck. David lands punch after punch onto the man. Nothing seems to work; getting frustrated, the man yells out, standing up again. He reaches down to his belt, grabbing a holstered weapon. Knowing what is does, David attempts to stop him from taking it out. The man will not quit. Joseph yells to David to do something. As David wrestles with his arm, quickly only one thought comes to mind. Throwing his leg as far back as he can, David swings it forward as hard as he can. The base of his shin lands right between the man's legs. For a brief moment, it feels as if everything stops as the three realize what David did. The man's voice groans out a few octaves higher than his normal deep voice. The muscles relax as he loses all concentration, allowing Joseph to tighten his grip. After a minute, the man falls to his knees, then flat on his face. Joseph finally lets go; the two have defeated the mountain of a man.

Sitting on the ground, the two take heavy deep breaths, recovering from the fight. David rubs his face, accessing his pain along with any potential injuries. Joseph looks over his fists and rubs his stomach for a few seconds.

"You know, Dave, that was pretty dirty," Joseph comments.

"Well, it's not like I had much of an option; I was using both hands and still losing to just one of his arms," David replies, pointing to the man.

"Yeah, it's hard to believe someone so large is human," Joseph says.

"He might give even the commander a run for his money," David murmurs.

"Ha, don't let him hear that; he might bury you alive," Joseph replies.

"Heh, maybe, anyway, let's check on Sam and Ben," David says while standing up.

David helps Joseph to his feet; the two then proceed through the back door. Entering the room, the two are stunned to find Sam and Ben loading their bags with gold bars. Looking around, they find shelves of gold along with bags filled with some kind of paper. Joseph opens a bag, looking inside, inspecting the paper notes. He asks Sam if either of them know what this is. She only responds, no, but she knows what gold is so they're taking as much as they can. Quickly, Joseph and David begin loading their bags full of the gold as well. Full to the brim, the four begin their swift escape. Going all the way back to the first room, Joseph creaks open the front door. Looking out, he sees the people have gotten the fire under control. This means, less people are running around in panic; they are sitting around now, watching. Closing the crack in the door, Joseph notifies the group that getting out will be harder than getting in. The only idea they can come up with is a quick rush across, then back into the sand dunes. They agree to sprint out on three. One. Two. Three. They swing the door open; standing in the middle of the street, a group of men are waiting, looking at the group who has just swung open the front door, holding a lot of what is presumably their money. Quickly, the group rush back through the door, as the men begin taking out their weapons. As the door closes, the men use their weapons, ripping the face of the building. The four quickly dive to the ground, crawling around in an attempt to take cover. Soon, the weapons stop; all goes quiet. Then one man begins yelling out, but the four can't understand what he's saying. Stuck in the room, there is no other way out; all the windows are barred shut. There is no escape; they talk about what to do.

"I say, we hand over the stuff and maybe they'll let us go," Sam says.

"First off, I didn't just fight a mountain to leave empty-handed. Second, they just attacked us without a word. These people don't come off as that reasonable; I doubt they'll let us go," Joseph responds.

"I sort of agree with Joseph; they come off as the hit first, ask later type of people," David remarks.

"Then, what do we do? I'm not dying here," Sam insists.

"If only there was a distraction or som—" Joseph is interrupted.

In the back of the building, an explosion blows out the back wall of the room they were in before. Looking through the door, they see men covering their faces in masks and jumping through the hole. They enter the room where the four had left some gold they couldn't carry. The four crawl to the corners of the front room as footsteps are heard outside. The door busts open; the men outside heard the commotion and rushed in. A fight ensues between the two groups of men. Unexpectedly the group from outside are more concerned about the fight than the four of them. Taking this opportunity, they begin crawling out of the door, under a hail of fire and smoke.

In the middle of the road, the four finally stand up to sprint back down the alleyway, past the homes, finally making it into the sand dunes. Above them, the sun bakes them like a hot oven, despite the sun slowly falling to the side as the day passes, this does nothing to quell the heat. For people who lived on a consistently wet island in the ocean, heat like this felt like fire. Spending too much time in this desert would be their end, they know it. However, being in an unfamiliar land with no direction, they can only keep marching. It feels like hours have gone by. Their feet that once left the sand, as they walk now, they drag, creating a rut that quickly collapses with sand. They need a way out, quickly anything; they even consider begging the monster for help. What would that thing care? It'd sooner kill them and steal their belongings. Argument after argument—the heat forces the worst out of them. Their only saving grace appears in the distance. A rock formation standing alone in the vast desert. It being the only source of shade around, they gather energy to sprint toward it. Crossing the line of sun to shade, they collapse into the sand. Even though the shade only provides a small amount of respite, it is a welcome time of rest reguardless. The air is still just as hot, but not being in direct sunlight is a boon to their energy. Taking a few minutes, they simply breathe lying in the sand. Their moment of rest is interrupted by a shaking of the ground. Sitting up, they look out to the dunes, thinking something is coming toward them. However, their suspicions of something coming are soon dismayed. Quickly, the horizon line of the dunes begin to rise up above them; confused, they soon realize it's them that's falling. Before they could do anything, they find themselves swallowed whole by the sand. A quick moment of eating nothing but sand, it spits them out into a large cavern. The only two sources of light is the small hole they fell through, along with their lanterns illuminating parts of the walls and any objects around them. It appears that the room is not that large. The ceiling stands a few feet above them, Joseph unhooks his lantern, raising it up to look at the ceiling better. Above them, is a structure of metal beams going in all directions. In the middle of these beams, there appears to be something confusing to the group.

"Glass?" Joseph confoundedly says.

"That's sand on top of glass alright," Sam says, confirming Joseph.

"Why are we in an underground room with glass?" asks David.

"Why are we in a desert carrying gold?" retorts Joseph.

"Fair point," David says. "Anyway, it seems the walls are stone," David continues.

"Yeah, but it's not like the rough stone we have," Sam says as she touches the wall.

"What do you mean?" asks David.

"Just come feel it; it's smooth with perfect squares in between these little grooves," Sam points out as she walks along the wall.

"Hmm, well my best guess is that different people have different building styles. But why was the town made of wood?" David contemplates, thinking of all kinds of questions.

"Either way, we're here so let's see what lies further down," Joseph tells them as he finds a doorway.

Walking through the doorway, they can go either left or right. However, walking forward, they come to a railing. This railing prevents them from falling into a large chasm. Picking up a stone, David drops it into the hole. As they listen, minutes go by; finally it lands with an echoing thud. They look at each other thinking the same thing; falling is not a good idea. Their only way forward is left or right, so they decide to go right. Following the pathway, they come across door after door. Soon, they see light coming from a room ahead. Peering around the corner, they see the familiar sight of a small waterfall of sand. It's the room they entered in; they groan in mild irritation. David tells them to wait here, then jogs off to the left—the way they came. After a quick minute, he appears on the other side of them to the right. It's a giant circle, they realize. Perhaps, one of the doors holds the way out they think. As they walk along, they open every door they can. However, they all hold the same thing: a room with glass above them caged in stone. Finally, after a good amount of doors, they come to one with two doors splitting in the middle. Opening one is a staircase, only heading down. They ponder for a moment if down is the best course of action. However, it would seem that they have no other option. Keeping the optimism going, David suggests that they might need to go down to come up somewhere else. They can only hope so.

Descending the short stairs, they come to a platform. Turning around to the left is another set of stairs going down. Following them leads to another set of two doors, or again behind them, to the left, more stairs. Curious, they open one door, only to find themselves one level lower in the same circular room. Thinking its best to not waste time, they continue down the stairs. Going down one set after another, after a while, they begin to take regular interval breaks. Their legs are burning, tired, and shaking. Resting just a minute can only do so much for their stamina. Thankfully, they reach a final platform; no more stairs; only a final set of doors. On their side, a metal pole is jammed through the door handles, barring the door from opening. Sliding the bar out, they make a final push to open the door. During their journeys, the group has seen as well as experienced quite a lot. However, the implications of this scene come off as disturbing. Littering the floor in groups lay skeletons, human remains, both tall and short. Among them, there lay even skeletons small enough to be infants. Carefully, they step over the dried skeletons draped in some white coats. Along the wall, they find signs of desperation from these people's final moments.

"The stone walls are all scratched," Sam points out.

"You mean they tried to claw their way out?" David asks.

"Mm, it looks like it; the back of the metal door is scratched too," Sam continues.

"Obviously they didn't really get far, huh," Joseph says as he walks to the other side of the room.

"No, but they tried with nothing but their hands," David murmurs as he kneels down.

"Who knows what went on here, but their final moments were clearly not good," Sam says.

"Well, it looks like someone tried something else than getting out," Joseph states, holding his lamp to the wall.

"What do you mean?" David asks as he stands up.

"Come and try to make sense of this drawing," Joseph calls them over.

Etched into the wall is a mural of sorts. The person who drew it decided to leave words out, only focusing on the art. In the very center is a crude drawing of what might be where they are. It depicts the long center chasm with the floors around it. Shooting from the top of the hole, a long pillar propelled by fire. Up above the pillar is an identical one; however, this one is in pieces, engulfed in flame. Next to all this is another drawing of their current position. This time filled with little stick drawing of people filling the bottom. Outside the hole are angry looking stick figures holding weapons. The people are being pushed into the hole, then the door is locked tight. The final mural starts some circle, but as it would have happened, the artist had died before finishing it.

"What does it all mean?" Sam asks.

"This is only a guess, but it looks like the people here made some contraption to go up. Maybe into the sky or even further, but ultimately it failed," David explains.

"But then why were they forced down here?" Sam asks again.

"Perhaps punishment for their failure; I don't know; we can only guess," David replies.

"Well, it's not like we can do anything for the people; so let's find a way out," Joseph says while walking away along the wall.

Soon, Joseph finds another set of two doors. He pulls on them, but they don't budge. So Joseph pushes again; the doors refuse to move. Joseph calls the rest over to where he is to help open the door. All together, they pull on the handles. The handle David and Sam were holding onto breaks off, sending them backwards to the ground. The two get up, dusting themselves off, getting ready to try again. One more time, they all push on the door, hoping it opens. For now, the door may as well just be a wall. Taking a moment to breathe, they talk about other alternatives. During this conversation, Joseph has a small fit of anger and he kicks the door, yelling at it to open. To the shock of everyone, it does; the door flings open inwards away from them. They stare at one another before looking through the door. All they can see is solid darkness; the type of darkness they're all too familiar with.

"Guess, we got our way home," David comments.

Joseph simply replies as he walks through, "Yeah, guess we do."

CHAPTER 21

FACADE

As they drop their four bags of gold onto the table outside the gate, it nearly collapses from the combined weight. The young girl sitting at the table is astonished for a brief moment. She pushes her glasses back up into her face, as if to not believe this sight in front of her. "Well then," are the only words to escape her mouth as she pulls up her book. Opening it halfway, she begins reading through a few lines. After a few lines, she pulls out a pen, then begins writing. Just a handful of numbers in, she looks back up, telling them to go get food as this will take a while. Shrugging, the group can only wait, adding the fact that they are exhausted; they take this chance to get real rest.

Sitting down in the cafeteria, David nervously checks the time: 11:27. He thinks to himself for a moment. If the girl works fast enough, he might be able to buy the cure before the day is over. Planning his route, David would have to go back to the tree to collect his savings, then run around the island to the other side, buy the cure, then run back home. However, first David knows he needs rest along with food. Collecting a plate of food, David quietly sits back down to eat. Sam excitedly talks about the prospects of owning her own store. She talks of names, items to sell, even locations to set up. Ben sits quietly, happily acknowledging he'd support her. As their conversation goes on and on, David has finished his food. Setting the fork and knife down, he sits his head back against the chair. The wave of exhaustion washes over him, along with the relief that this will all be over.

The cracking of fire fills the air; the dim light of multiple fires are dancing all around. David soon shoots his eyes open, realizing he had fallen asleep. Quickly, he pulls out his watch one more time: 2:18. Looking around, he sees he is alone among the few who are also asleep at the cafeteria. Standing up, he runs to the collection tent; the table is empty and abandoned. Standing watch outside of the tent are two guards. He goes up to one, pleading to let him talk to the girl to collect his money. They simply wave him off, telling him to come back in the morning. It's urgent, he says, he doesn't want it he needs it; he implores them again and again, even going so far as to get on his knees; the guards are speechless. Witnessing such a commotion go on, their faces are full of pity soon. The tent flaps open, the girl walks out, rubbing her eyes. She asks what's all the noise about. Her eyes are finally wide enough to see David on the floor, begging for his money. David is explaining he had fallen asleep, but the girl interrupts him. Holding up two thick envelopes, she tells him that she found him asleep, so she decided to hold onto the money for him. Before even taking the money, he profusely thanks her over and over. She simply tells him to take it, letting her get back to sleep. Taking the envelopes, David sprints off, kicking up dirt behind him. Running to the dock, David jumps over fire pits people have made that are in his way, coming to groups of people David finds a way to get in between the people standing around, shoving them if need be, but still apologizing as he runs off. Reaching the beach, he makes his way to the final boat; the captain is asleep at the wheel. David doesn't even wait for the door to fall down; instead chooses to jump up and over the wall. As he falls down into the boat, it rocks slightly; the sleeping captain rocks a tiny bit to the side before David appears behind him, shaking his shoulder, yelling for him to wake up. The captain jolts straight up, yelling, "That was his fish," before realizing he is no longer dreaming. David once again pleads for the captain to bring him home. Talking about the money, his mother, how much time he has. Confused, the captain tells him to calm down, then asks for fifty dollars. David pulls out a one hundred, telling the captain to keep the rest. The captain frowns slightly, whispering to himself, he should have asked for more. However, a deal is a deal; the captain kicks the engine into gear, chugging away into the lake.

David consistently checks his watch, so much so he might as well not stop watching it. 2:48, 2:49, 2:50. David watches the minutes tick by. 3:02. They dock on the ocean; again in anticipation, David climbs the front wall. As he climbs, he thanks the man again multiple times before falling over it, onto the dock. The captain yells out calling him crazy but can only watch his back as David runs up the ramp. Sighing, he simply whispers, "Kids." David runs down the alleyways, dodging trash on the ground and the few people clogging his way, passing shops, factory, and homes; one person who was leaving nearly opened the door into David's face. However, he notices it just in time to move to the side, avoiding it. Panting and out of breath, David stands at the bottom of the stairs to the tree: 3:25. One step at a time, David ascends upwards in what felt like no time at all; David has risen above the city. Standing on the top of the hill, flashes of light from out in the ocean start to appear. Looking out at the storm, David grins, whispering that no storm could ruin today.

On both knees, David digs away at the dirt under the tree, moving rocks to the side, finally hitting his metal box. Uncovering it, David stands up excited; he fumbles with the locks until he pops them open. Ready to do a final count of all his money, he lifts the lid. Peering down into the box, David's hope and excitement quickly die. "No, no, no." David throws the empty box to the ground. He falls to his knees again, digging away, in refusal of reality. "It is somewhere here, it has to be," David says over and over to himself. Nearly both of his arms are deep in nothing but a dirt hole. In David's lapse of thinking, he throws his head into the ground, yelling out in pain, but more so in agony of his lost possessions. Tears stream from David's eyes, down his face, as he grits his teeth in anger, sadness, and frustration. Too many emotions at one time, all stinging worse than the last.

All this time, all this hardship for nothing but an empty box! His only comforting dullness of the pain is punching the ground, damning the world.

As David's feelings subside, thoughts start to make an appearance. Why, was obvious; someone found money, then took it. Who, was the difficult question. No one ever comes up this hill, no one would have known. A revelation comes to David's mind. Silently, all movement stops; David's thoughts and yelling quiet down. Slowly, he turns his head over to the side. Just enough for one eye to gaze out over the whole island. One word escapes, one name comes to mind.

Joseph.

Pushing himself out of the dirt, clumps fall off his face. The only light illuminating the early morning are flashes of lightning. Without uttering another word, David slowly takes one step after another down the stairs, these old shaky cobblestone steps, overgrown with grass and dirt. Halfway down, David begins jogging down, occasionally skipping a step to go faster. Factories and homes take over the view. The sky is still dark before the sunrise. Landing at the last step, David begins sprinting, shoving anything, anyone out of his way. Alleyway after alleyway, street after street, David appears before the two guards once again. 5:30. With a hushed tone, full of anger, David demands to be let through the gate. The guards look down at David; the first time they met, he appeared timid, scared even. Now his personality has made a one-eighty; despite the size difference, now the guards are the one filled with fear. Timidly, one guard opens the gate quietly, letting David through. Rushing past District 10, David once again finds himself at the foot of Joseph's door. With rage, he pounds on the door with his fist, yelling out to Joseph to open the door. Waiting a minute, a tired Joseph, half asleep, opens the door. Seeing David, he starts off his usual greeting.

"Oh, hey, Da—" Joseph is interrupted by David's fist landing square on his chin.

"You stole Mom's money, my money," David yells at Joseph lying on the floor. "Where's the money; gi—" David pauses. Pointing straight at David is the barrel of the weapon the giant man had from the last dive. "Why do you have that?" David asks in a hushed tone.

"To be better; we saw what these did to people. How could a sword compare?" Joseph replies. "While you were sleeping earlier, I thought of something; why stop. There's more than money in there, there's power, power our money can't buy. Now, I'm going to give you the option; continue diving with me or get out," Joseph says as he waves the barrel toward the door.

"Why bother diving anymore? You killed Mom," David replies as his eyes begin tearing up.

"She had no need for the money anyway; it all belongs to me," Joseph says.

His comment enrages David, making him take a step forward. However, Joseph again emphasizes the weapon into David's face.

With no other alternative, David turns around quietly toward the door. He leaves, closing the door to Joseph. Down the steps, David turns for one last look. Just between the crack of the door, they lock eyes. David didn't notice before because of the heat of the moment, but in this moment, Joseph's eyes were not blue. All color looked as if it had abandoned them; they were hollow and black. However, David has to make a plea for the cure now, hoping the money he has at hand will be a decent down payment. David goes to Joseph's neighbor, knocking on the door. After a minute, there's no answer; knowing there are more homes, he goes to the next. Then David goes to the next, the next, the next; no one is answering. Doing his best to dodge the downpour of rain, district after district, David finds himself all the way up to the last house in District 1. The top of the top, the largest, most prestigious house on the island. Surrounded by trees, trimmed hedges, water fountains, but not a soul. David pounds against the door; nothing happens. None of the homes answered, not even a butler, a maid, the groundskeeper. Panicking, David slams against the door, doing everything to get some reaction. After a few shoves of his body against the door, it breaks off the hinges. David collapses inside, finally hoping to find someone. Look's up ,David sees, nothing but a home. More accurate, the skeleton of a house. Looking down the hallway, through doors into rooms, he sees there's nothing, not a table, painting, rug, couch; the only light source is the flashes of lightning coming through the windows. Running out, David goes back a district to the next closest house. Breaking the door down again, David finds the same thing. Nothing, no furnishings, no sign of life, no one lives here. No one does anything here; this is all, fake. Standing on the steps, David, in shock, can only look out at the island with a blank face. The heavy rain washes over everything. Why is this here? Why is this all like this? If no one is here, then who can he buy the cure from. Is there a cure? David stands there, his world collapsing in, the rain bringing a weird silence to everything. 6:00. The morning gong rings out three times as it always does.

CHAPTER 22

THE FINAL DIVE

Drenched, David walks down the roads back home. The rain a never ending torrent. Unfazed, he even walks through columns of rain spilling over from gutters. His march feels like an eternity, but it's not too long before he finds himself home. Looking up at the creaking, broken building, David can only feel how empty it's going to be. Opening the door, David turns the corner, dripping water everywhere, all over the floor. David's mother, still in her wheelchair, is looking out the window. He quietly shuffles his feet across the floorboards. Standing behind her, David leans down, placing his head on her shoulder.

After a moment, she coughs, and with a dry course voice she speaks, "Why are you wet, David?"

"It's raining," David quietly replies.

"What were you doi—" she coughs for a moment, "doing in the rain?"

"Nothing, just coming home," David responds in a sullen voice. Soon, he begins crying into her shoulder. "I'm sorry. I'm so sorry, Mom, we wasted everything."

"What do you mean?" his mother asks.

"I almost had the money for your cure; Joseph stole it, but it doesn't even matter. There is no cure to buy, there's no one to sell it. Everything was worthless; all the while, we kept lying to you. Me and Joseph were diving, going through the gate. We kept going into the abyss," David pauses to collect himself as he cries.

"I know, I know," his mother comforts him.

David stops to look up, to look his mother in the eyes. "You know? How did you know?" he asks, puzzled.

"Call it a mother's instinct; I never said anything because it wouldn't have changed anything. It's not like I would have been able to stop either of you anyway," she drifts her eyes down. Her body is stone hard from the neck down, covered in gray, craggy rocks on the surface. "I can't even console my son as he cries."

Rubbing the tears and snot from his face, David replies. "Just the fact that you're here is enough to console me, Mom; I just wish life was different."

"That would be nice, but I can feel it; I'm not here for much longer," she pauses; just below her chin, the rocks creep closer up, cracking and shattering, new rock forms. "So go; Joseph still lives; he may not be himself but he's in there somewhere inside himself. He's your only family now; he's your only brother. Do everything you can," she begins to dry heave and cough. She then gives one final yell, "Do everything to drag him back out to the light."

Silently, David stands up and walks in front of his mother. Looking down, he can see the last bits of determination in her eyes. David wipes his face one last time, leans down for a hug, and kisses her cheek. Leaning back up, they share a final quiet goodbye. He then runs to the front door, collecting his tools. Throwing the door open, David is faced with a storm unlike anything they have seen. Wind and rain in all directions, whipping and tearing, pieces of homes flying off. Undaunted, David runs down to the dock. The water is wild, crashing against the land, rocking the solitary boat back and forth. The captain is doing his best to tie it down to the dock.

Coming up to him, David asks for a ride to the island. The man calls him crazy for wanting to go now, denying him. David pulls out his two full fat envelopes of money.

"Then, I'll buy your boat," David says

Looking at the envelopes, the man knows his boat is worth one quarter of his offer. Nonetheless, he takes the offer, still letting David know that he's insane.

"Maybe," David replies as he jumps into the boat.

Doing his best to stay standing, David keeps leaning side to side, while the boat is doing its best to throw him off. Getting to the back wall, David clings onto to the top; doing small jumps, he pulls himself up. Rolling over, he falls into the captain's chair. Sitting up, he adjusts his position, wiping water away from his eyes. David stares down at the controls, confused; only a handful are labeled. He tries to think of the many times he watched them pilot these boats. First, he needs the engines on; looking at the panel, he finds a key. As it's already inserted, he turns it to the side. The engines begin kicking to life, sputtering and shooting water from the exhaust. Feeling the key force its way back, David lets go of it. Determined, David turns the key again; now explosions begin coming from the exhaust. A small flame shoots out before the key kicks back once again.

"Come on, come on," David whispers for a third time, turning the key.

One large pow and the engines roar to life. Knowing it's too early to celebrate, David looks around again for what to do next. Going forward is a good place to start. Thankfully, one of the things labeled is a lever that can go forward or backwards and is labeled as such. Shoving the whole lever forward, the engines roar and rock but the boat refuses to move. Panicking, David frantically looks over the panel, touching nobs, buttons; nothing feels like it will move. Soon, David's hand lands on a lever next to the chair. Pulling the small trigger on it, the lever falls down forward. The boat jerks forward, finally moving across the water. Unsure of what speed to go at or even how to gauge it, David simply leaves it on full throttle, moving at a speed he never thought the boats would move. David takes this solitary moment to bask in it all. Even with all the rain, wind, and violent rocking of the boat, David found a semblance of peace in it all. At this point in the lake, the storm has covered everything. David is surrounded by nothing, for a brief moment; he even hears nothing. Not for long, however; the few flickering lights of campfires start to emerge in the distance. Back in reality, David swiftly pulls the speed lever back into reverse. However, the momentum carries David onwards. Frantically, he pulls the lever down by the seat all the way up. Using both of his arms, he gets it locked into place. Now the engines begin whirring down; none of it matters, the boat is still moving too fast. David hunches up, bracing himself. The front of the boat slams into the beach, launching the front up and forward. Quickly, it crashes back down; the momentum, still with enough force, slides the boat across the sand, coming to a halt, just steps away from the commander's tent. David, slightly beaten and bruised, picks himself up back into the seat. Rubbing his head with one hand, he slowly turns the key off with his other hand. The engines calm down as they begin shutting off.

"What was all that noise?" the commander shouts, opening the tent flap. "What the?" Just a few steps away, the front end of a boat sits staring him down.

David rolls over the top of the console, flopping down to the ground. "Sorry, I'll fix it later," David yells as he gets up, then runs off.

"Kid? That you, what happened?" the commander shouts back under the noise of the storm.

"Sorry," David yells out again, his response muffled by the storm.

Running through the camp, David nearly hits multiple people. His vision is obscured by the rain, but he knows this layout like the back of his hand. Tent after tent, David blindly makes his way to the gate. Standing just in front of the opening, David stares up at the stone. Looking over the inlays, cracks, and small holes, David is filled with the same feeling he had when he first stood here. However, it is different now; David draws his sword, thrusting the tip toward the gate.

"You're not stopping me from getting my brother back," David charges in, one last time.

Sprinting down the initial hallway, David comes to the first set of open doors. Twenty stand before him. Looking over them all, David has to make a decision where to go. Only one of the doors is where Joseph went in, but which one. As he observes them, there is no indication of which one is correct. David has to make a decision, but which one, which would Joseph choose? Closing his eyes, David makes a blind choice, running into one of the doors, yelling out in frustration. The first room he comes to is overgrown with plants, even trees litter the area. Shoving his way through, David hacks at any bushes or plants in his way to make it to the other side. Pulling himself through the dark forest, David emerges on the other side; another door is open and waiting. With no time to waste or think, David runs through the door. Emerging on the other side, he finds himself in a burned down home. Kicking the door open, he finds another room in the home. He then finds another door; swinging it open is another room. It's a maze of rooms. David opens door after door, room after room. Soon, he finally finds a door; rushing through, he falls into a pit of mud. Grabbing his sword next to him, David stands back up. Looking around, nothing of note can be seen, just mud below him. Picking his knees up to his chest to walk, David slowly finds a hollowed-out dirt hallway. As he trudges down the hallway with each step, the mud slowly begins to solidify. Now, as he makes way, the mud turns to dried dirt; the dirt crumbles and cracks, turning into sand. Somehow still in the abyss, the sand begins getting carried by the wind, blasting David from all directions. He emerges from the sandstorm, covered in sand, mud, sticks, and leaves stuck to him. David finds Joseph standing before him, about to open another door.

"Joseph!" David yells. Freezing, Joseph stops; quickly he turns around, drawing out the weapon he pointed at David before. "Stop this, it's madness; you aren't you, Joseph, let's go home," David pleas to find some semblance of his brother.

Joseph opens his mouth but the voice coming out is not his; its deep, guttural sounds, as if multiple people speak as one. "It's mine, it's all mine. Everything belongs to me. Gold, silver, diamonds, emeralds, EVERYTHING! And when I finish here, your brother will be mine; we, will, be, one. When I get out of here, I will get my revenge," the monster controlling Joseph forces him to pull the trigger of the weapon.

Expecting a loud bang, David flinches. However, nothing happens; David opens his eyes, looking at Joseph. Joseph, in turn, looks at the gun, confused; realigning it at David again, he pulls the trigger again. Nothing, so again, again, again, again. No smoke, no bang, just a fancy paper weight. Taking this moment of confusion as opportunity, David rushes at Joseph, tackling him; the two fall through the door. Rolling onto the ground, they enter a strangely well-lit room. Looking around, they see pillars decorate both sides of a walkway, illuminated by standing torches. Down the walkway at the end, some square box is closed, lying on the ground; it is both tall and wide enough for a person to fit into. Confused, David has questions; however, more urgent matters are present. Turning his back to the box, David faces Joseph, who unsheathes his golden sword, throwing the sheath to the side. The fire light flickers and dances on the golden shine, reflecting small shimmers of light around the room. Not a single imperfection touches the sword; the blade perfectly straight, the edge immaculate. In contrast, David's sword has a slight bend in the body and the edge is dulled and dented in places. Scratches line the sword in every manner as well. But this is David's sword; it has carried him this far, it shall carry him just a little further.

David stands perfectly still; his muscles tense, the handle of the sword poised just at his waist. The blade of the sword come upwards at a forty-five-degree angle, the tip just at eye level. Sadly, David had only recently gotten into training his sword skills, while only testing himself once or twice in combat. Joseph, on the other hand, had gained interest in the sword from the beginning, testing his skills many times. Opposed to David, Joseph stood quite relaxed, confident in his ability. Joseph hung his sword to the side in a fashion that he could almost use it as a cane. He knows where his sword is at all times, like an extension of his body; holding a sword is natural for him. Nonetheless, David has to make a move; staring at Joseph will not change anything. David takes a step forward. Joseph doesn't react at all. After a few steps, David's sword is just an arm's reach away from Joseph.

From here, David flicks his wrists down, bringing the sword with it. In one swift motion, Joseph brings his sword up, slapping David's sword to the side. Joseph's blade comes hurdling at David's head. Quickly, David pulls the handle up, the tip facing the floor; the blades clash, sending sparks flying in all directions. David's poor block sends him staggering a step back. But there is no time; the second assault begins. Joseph thrusts the tip of the sword at David's gut. David attempts to smack it away to create an opening. However, Joseph is much faster, drawing the sword back to his chest. David's sword hits nothing but air; his swing goes too far. Joseph takes advantage of the opening again, bringing the sword straight down. Just in the nick of time, David rotates his torso, forcing his sword to move a little faster. Fast enough to clash against the sword once more, the force sends David back another step. Both swords up in the air, David having faster momentum does his best to copy the same strike, bringing his sword straight down. Joseph simply twists his body, letting the sword fall right past him to the ground. Too close together, Joseph with his free hand, lands a punch across David's face. The unexpected hit sends David back another step. David is in a retreating fight, and he knows it; he needs an upper hand, anything. While he's thinking, however, Joseph swings his sword from the ground upwards. David's sword in no position to counter, Davids only option is to jump backwards. Sitting on the ground, David is open to any number of attacks. Joseph chooses the simplest; again he reverses the swing up to now face down. David scoots back, spreading his legs, letting the sword clash on the ground. Thinking of the punch, David raises a leg, planting his foot square on Joseph's face, kicking him back. Disoriented, Joseph rubs his face, then looks over to David, notably more angry than he was before. David quickly looks around for anything to use but comes to the realization that the monster came to this room for a reason. Box, the large box, David thinks, hit it, cut it, destroy the box, destroy the monster. He doesn't need to win against Joseph in a fight, just against the monster. Standing up, David readies his sword again. In anger, Joseph swings the sword from the right side. David moves his sword to block. They clash; David steps back again as another attack comes from the left, horizontal swipe, David blocks again; sparks fill their faces and David is forced again to step back. Joseph lets out a flurry of blow after blow, right, left, right, left. The monster has had its fun and intends to end this one way or another, throwing all technique out the window. After all, with someone with such a low skill level, what would you need such technique for anyway.

Soon, just as David wanted, he had made enough of a retreat backwards to reach the steps up to the box. He needs an opening to get up them, so he waits for another block, then swings his sword down. As they collide in the air, David forgoes his stance, bringing one foot up again, kicking Joseph in the stomach. The two fall backwards; David onto the steps, Joseph onto the floor. Quickly, David turns to run up the multitude of steps to reach the box. Looking up the steps, Joseph notices David's end goal. Yelling out to stop, he reaches an arm out to the side and swipes it to David. From the darkness, a large black tendril shoots out, slamming into the back side of one of the large pillars. As it falls, the flame light touches the tendril; it sizzles and hisses as it returns to the darkness. It achieved its goal of knocking the pillar down regardless. With great force, the pillar comes crashing down just behind David at the base of the stairs. For a moment, it bounces back up just a little, then settles on the ground. The whole floor begins to shake, and the pillar starts falling onto the floor. Following suit, the stone and rubble, the floor under their feet, collapse into a massive chasm. The hole is just large enough to engulf the two of them. They both cling to their suggested slabs of stone as they descend into a free fall. Thinking the fall is the most of his problems, David clings to any crack he can for dear life. Landing just in front of him, Joseph has jumped from one rubble to the other, looking to continue the fight. "Come on," is the only thing David groans out as he begins to stand, bracing his sword once again. Standing on a large free-falling platform, David has no more room to maneuver back. It's time to stand firm, as firm as he can on a falling rock, continuing a sword fight.

Not knowing just how long they might fall for, David makes his attempts to end this fast now. He steps forward, turning his wrists to the side, letting the sword fall over to the side. Quickly, he flicks his wrists forward, then follows through, swinging the sword diagonally upwards. Joseph leans back, letting the sword pass him by. As David overswings the sword, Joseph grabs his wrists with his free hand. Securing David's defense, Joseph raises his sword up to come down again. In the split-second, David's first instinct was to pull away, but he decides to shove himself into Joseph. This closes the gap between the two, causing Joseph's hand to hit David's shoulder instead of the blade. David twists his hands further away, releasing Joseph's grasp, then forces the bottom of the handle toward Joseph's face. Joseph turns, letting David's hands fly by, but for a moment, he forgets about the sword. David follows through, just about to land a hit on Joseph; however, Joseph raises his sword up along his head. Instead of cutting Joseph's face, David's sword cuts along the edge of Joseph's sword, protecting him. When David's sword passes, Joseph shoves David away, creating another gap for him to swing the sword diagonally down at David. David quickly ducks down, letting the sword pass over him. Joseph's knee comes up, landing a blow straight to David's face, sending his back up right. In the reverse now, Joseph draws his sword back in the same diagonal direction now with David in its path. David turns his sword up, then turns on his feet, letting the swords slash against each other. Joseph draws his sword up, the handle to the side of his face, blade pointed outwards towards David, Joseph thrusts the sword toward David in one fluid motion. David leans back Joseph's sword in between him and his own sword. Pushing to the side, Joseph swipes the sword toward David. David quickly steps back again and again, moving with the sword, doing his best to keep it away from him. David's foot finds a crack in the ground, making him trip back. As he does, Joseph with his sword slaps David's sword in the other direction, freeing it from his hands. David, now sitting on the ground defenseless, looks up at Joseph as he raises his sword for another strike. Loud crashing is heard around them from the other falling debris; Joseph staggers for a moment, looking around, then finally back at David on the slab of stone, then darkness.

Coughing, David waves the dust from his face as he lies on the ground just on the outer part of the circle of light emanating from Davids lantern that had detached itself from his waist. Crawling over the various rocks, David digs himself out from broken debris. Picking up the lantern, David kneels, looking around, getting a sense for his direction, and to find Joseph. In the distance, a faint glow can be seen; it's most likely Joseph's lantern. Climbing down, David stumbles his way over, tripping every so often on some group of rocks. Coming into the light, he sees Joseph is sitting back against a large rock, his legs stretched out to either side. Right in the center of his chest is Joseph's own sword, impaling him straight through, with the other half of the sword coming out his back, embedded into the large stone.

"No!" David yells out. "No, no, no, no," David repeats as he falls over to Joseph's side.

"My vessel, broken, my plan halted," the monster mutters. "Why do you still live!" the monster groans out, looking up. "It appears I made the wrong gamble," the monster whispers, looking down at the sword wound. At first, there is no blood spilling out, but a black inky sludge. It bubbles and spews out from the opening; the monster yells out in rage from Joseph's mouth. As the black sludge keeps flowing, the darkness from Joseph's eyes start to fade. The monster's yell slowly subsides to its original owner's voice, Joseph's voice. Looking up, Joseph smiles, then mutters one thing, "David."

"Joseph! Joseph, I'm sorry, I wanted to drag you out of here, not hurt you," David begins crying over his brother.

"No, it's my fault, Dave. I wasn't in control of myself. I watched everything happen; I couldn't stop anything," Joseph says as he places a hand on David's cheek. "I'm the one who should apologize." Joseph takes a large wheeze in, before continuing, "I started this, and I never meant for it to get like this."

"It's fine, it's fine, I-I'll get you out," David pulls on the sword embedded into the rock; however, it refuses to move.

"Dave, Dave!" Joseph yells out, waving David to stop. "You can't, even if you did, I can't walk, I can't feel my legs and I'm bleeding too much. I'll just be dead weight."

"Don't talk like that; I can drag you out, I promised Mom I would," David continues pulling the sword.

"I said," Joseph wheezes again, "Stop!" Joseph grabs David's hands, pulling him down. David kneels in front of Joseph, thumping his head into Joseph's chest, crying. "You want to make us proud, right? You did your best, get out of here; don't come back, live a full happy life. I left all my money in a chest in my house; take it, and you won't have to struggle anymore."

David quietly nods, all the while still sobbing into Joseph's chest.

"Good," Joseph wheezes one more time. "Take my lamp, with the two of them you should be able to get out; follow the compass."

David unhooks the lantern from Joseph's belt raising it up next to both of their faces.

"Don't worry, wherever we go when we die, I'll apologize to Mom and take the brunt of the punishment," Joseph softly smiles. "Go."

A loud roar fills the space they're in; the monster has come back to what it once was and begins declaring, "YOU! WILL! NOT! LEAVE! HERE!"

Joseph pushes David away. "GO! Now," he urges David to start running.

David locks eyes one last time with his brother; as the light slowly fades, Joseph is consumed by the darkness. A loud crash from where David just was can be heard, followed by an agonizing yell, "AAARRRRRRGGGGHHH!" the monster is not happy. With no other alternative, David pulls out his compass, following the arrow.

"YOU WERE NOTHING MORE THAN A COG." Slamming and destruction can be heard all around David as he runs. "YOU HAD NO LARGER ROLE TO PLAY IN MY PLAN." David frantically runs as fast as his legs can carry him, as the loud thumping gets only closer and closer in the darkness. "YOU WILL DIE."

David diligently follows the arrow as it moves from side to side, slightly changing direction. The light, keeping David safe, slowly starts to lose its confidence. Out of the corner of his eyes, now and then, the black tendrils of the monster can be seen. It's doing its best to choke the life out of the light to make its way closer. Some tendrils even sacrifice themselves, launching out into the light to knock the lantern free from David. However, David keeps a tight grip on the lantern, not letting the barrage of sizzling charred tendrils stop him. Strangely, the stomping has caused the ground to start giving way, creating more and more holes to somehow fall even deeper. Finally, the door can be seen; it's just on the other side of a large hole; the door is suspended in the air. With no other direction and the stomping getting closer and closer, David has to jump. Mustering all his energy, David leaps out, stretching his arms as far as they can. Following just behind him, large tendrils, the size of David, whip out in a final attempt to grab him. However, David's fingertip just brushes the door, sending him hurdling down into the hole. The black tendril crashes into the door, letting out a final yell as David fades into the darkness, "NOOOOOOOOOOOO!"

Shocked by the sudden fall, even David lets out a yell, curling into a ball to protect himself. After a minute, he slowly calms down, coming to the realization that he is still alive. At the same time, he also notices that he doesn't get the feeling of falling anymore. Peaking one eye open, he sees that he is now lying on a floor; at least that's what he thinks. Pressing his hand down, he finds it is indeed a floor, but there is no floor to be seen. It's a strange empty blackness; littering all across the floor are these shimmering little lights. Peering down gives David the sense of looking up at the night sky, but it is not; he is looking down. It's notable as well; it's quiet, a strange stillness, quiet. The only sounds that break up this quiet is a strange ice shatter noise. A strange noise, like wherever David is, is fragile. Opening the other eye, David gets a better look. It's dark but not a consuming darkness. David can somehow see through it, without the need for the lantern. As David looks around, he sits up, then turns around for a better image of his surroundings. Towering over David is a strange statue. Standing up, he gets a better look at the statue. It's him; the statue is David in his current attire; it's as if what made this statue took David as he is now and carved it into a statue. The statue is full of all his details, even down to the cuts and scratches. "Why is this here? How did this get here? Where is here?" David asks out loud, hoping for an answer. But nothing, there is nothing to answer David. For a brief moment, David panics and tries to run in a direction. However, to no avail; some force keeps David right where he stands, even though his feet are touching the ground and moving. Stopping, David takes a breath once more, before yelling out in frustration.

"WHERE AM I!"